The Men

Fanny Calder

THE REAL PRESS

www.therealpress.co.uk

Published in 2016 by the Real Press,
www.therealpress.co.uk © Fanny Calder

ISBN (print) 978 0955226397

Cover design: Paul Cleary

To the men.

Some of whom I want to thank

D EATH terrifies me. It has done since I was six years old. I used to lie in bed pleading with God not to let our block of flats burn down while I was asleep.

As a teenager I lay in bed at night and imagined myself lifeless, beneath the earth, over. This panicked me so badly that I started believing in God again, hoping this time that I could negotiate an after-life for myself. I also thought about cloning myself as a way of getting life after death, but I didn't think that this was a satisfactory solution as my clone would not actually be me.

Towards the end of my first term at university, when snow covered old buildings and Christmas lights hung from the trees, something in me cracked and I could think of nothing but my own death for a whole appalling week. Nothing else at all. I can remember brushing my teeth and thinking of death, watching Christmas TV and thinking of death, eating pasta and thinking of death. The fear was with me until the moment I finally fell asleep at night and was waiting for me as soon as I woke up in the morning. I was trapped, cornered, insane. I went home to my mother who was kind but wouldn't take me seriously as she said she was looking forward to dying.

I recovered by looking at the large beech trees at the bottom of our lawn and thinking about their slow lives and the little deaths and rebirths that they suffered every year.

Later on, I met one other person who took death as seriously as I did. He was funny and clever and debonair but when he got very drunk he would howl in terror at the thought of it. I knelt beside him as he howled, stroking his head.

I came to see death as an ally. It was the most terrifying thing and I could look at it without flinching. In comparison, everything else that might have frightened me was trivial. So it made me brave.

Then I got caught up with the men and forgot all about it.

The Singer

I am eighteen. School is a glamorous maelstrom of hormones within which the songs he writes circulate like religious artefacts. Battered cassettes with the band's name handwritten on them. Track listings on the cardboard inserts also handwritten and grubby. Our own private rock and roll gods.

He leaves the school the year before I arrive so I hear him sing before I meet him. On the cassettes he sounds worn-down and sad. This is romantic.

I don't remember meeting him, but I remember going to a pub at the other end of town from school to see his band play. The sun went down on a summer evening and I found myself with a group of men drinking beer in the pub garden as we waited for the music to start. The men were large, sweaty, funny, their laughter generous. They were at ease with themselves in a way that the boys at school were not. I was thrilled by them.

I cannot remember meeting him, or that first performance.

But days or weeks later I remember the night of our leavers' dance. I wore a white strapless dress. It was warm and I walked bare shouldered with my friend Annabel towards the dance and then past it, glancing in at our friends through the open dining hall door then leaving them behind us. The green hills glowed softly as we walked to the pub to see him.

For years afterwards I dream anxiously about that missed dance.

I don't remember our first kiss but I know that I spent that night with him in his bed, the first entire night I ever spent with a man. I was moved by the gentle way in which he held me in his sleep but I was on edge the whole night. I could not sleep and I was terrified of waking him so I could not move. I could not sleep and I could not move and I had drunk too much so my head ached. I can remember the sound of the milk float arriving at dawn and the bleakness that came with feeling more exhausted than I ever had before.

Hours later he finally woke up and reached across to kiss me and I let him but I was too terrified to speak and left soon after, stiff with self-consciousness, still in the white dress.

We spent a few more nights together after that. I only remember one of them, at a rainy music festival. Four people died in the mud in front of the stage that day. Men were throwing full cans of beer across the crowd, opened so that they sprayed beer into the rain as they flew. Sometime that afternoon one of the flying cans hit me on my left temple and nearly knocked me out. By the time we went to bed, the rain was almost heavy enough to put out the fire that he had made. We kissed and did as much as it was possible to do to each other in a damp narrow single sleeping bag. It was impossible to tell what he thought of me, whether he even liked me, but again he held me kindly and kept me warm and this time I managed to sleep fitfully, wound around him in the small bag.

A few months later, I briefly kissed his brother in a sad basement in South London.

I don't remember any more than this about meeting him, but I do remember the songs that he wrote and sang. They were hauntingly brilliant.

The invitation reads:

Roses are red

But our lips are redder
Romance is dead
But cold beds are deader
Sugar is sweet
But we prefer wine
Love is a joke
But it passes the time

I am much older now and I am throwing a party. I throw parties because I want to make magic, to create a stage on which I can shine.

This party has a theme: the invitations instruct guests to *Dress as Your Fantasy of Yourself*. I am holding it in honour of the dress that I am wearing. An ancient tutu that I found hanging from the roof of a shop in an out-of-the-way part of the city. I am taller and broader than the original ballerina, so a lace has been added to the back. The dress is boned and sequinned and the skirts froth out around my waist.

It makes me a princess, a fairy, a bride. Admitting that I am drawn to these clichés makes me powerful. I roll from conversation to conversation, drink to drink, making people laugh at my fantasies.

The party is in my flat at the very centre of the
city. A large empty space, painted in neutral
colours and furnished with a few anonymous,
pretentious things that the rental company have
provided for me. In the daytime it feels barren but
it is perfect for a party. Plenty of space to dance
and a floor that wipes clean.

I know only half of the people here. A very tall
and beautiful man dressed all in black leather is
trying to flirt with a tiny Asian woman in a nun's
outfit. He has to stoop down so that she can hear
him over the David Bowie CD that is booming
from the stereo. I don't know either of them. But I
do know the devil with glued-on horns sprouting
from his bald temples and my best friend is
Popeye, his pregnant girlfriend Morticia Adams.
Her dress is skin-tight and long, her bump
magnificently on display, her black, black skin
glowing.

A week before I had half-recognized a young
man with long hair at a political drinks party. He
introduced himself. It was the Singer's brother.

I invited him to the party.

Two men that I know well and a Scandinavian
woman who I have never seen before have come

without costumes. Now they are drunk and want to dress up. They pull off their clothes and, as they do so, they wrap one another in toilet paper, mummifying themselves carefully so that only a small strip of bare flesh shows at any one time. All three are blonde, tanned, handsome. Despite the wrapping and unwrapping they seem wholesome. Everyone at the party half watches the erotic process. I encourage the wrappers laughingly then go back to talking, drinking, dancing.

The door buzzer sounds. I pick up the entryphone. It is the Singer's brother.

"I hope you don't mind but I've brought him with me".

They come in together, the brother jolly and affectionate, the Singer polite and tentative. I welcome them and feel suddenly that the party is a success because he is here.

I wheel around still talking and still drinking. Wheel into a conversation that the Singer is having with someone I vaguely know.

We are asked how we know each other.

I say: "We went to the same school".

He says: "But not at the same time".

I am drunk and so I am fearless so then I say: "We used to fuck sometimes."

The person who we are talking to asks: "Why did you stop?"

I say: "Because we were both too neurotic."

"Yes," the Singer says, staring at me intensely. "Yes that is exactly it." His voice cracks like he is telling a joke or about to cry. "Too neurotic. You're absolutely right."

The look on his face and the way he speaks make me feel that what I have said is important to him. I am surprised.

I wheel back into the party and start to dance. I feel him watching. I dance and play and laugh. I am unafraid, delighted to no longer be the stiff girl listening for the milkman. When I have exhausted myself with dancing, I lean against the window and look out onto the street. He comes to stand next to me and we kiss easily. I wheel off into the party again and a moment later I am not sure whether this has really happened.

My bedroom is wilder than the dance floor. Somebody has taken my mirror down from the wall and is using it to cut lines of cocaine – I don't mind, but don't need or want it.

The three blondes who were wrapping one another are locked in my bathroom together. The man with devil's horns breaks into the bathroom through a secret cupboard door, laughing hysterically as he does so. When the three emerge there are hand-marks high on the bathroom mirror, as if someone has been pinned against it. I am glad about this wildness.

I lie on my back on the floor, tutu spread out around me. I am too tired to speak, but I am discussed.

"What is she?"

"What isn't she?"

"I think a she's a bride."

"Not a bride. A *goddess.*"

My eyes closed, I recognize the Singer's voice.

At the end of the party three men remain. The Singer, his brother and a small man who has danced vigorously with me several times during the night. I am awake and upright again and I can tell that they all want to go to bed with me. I don't care about the small man, who is unattractive by dint of being both shy and aggressive. But I feel awkward about the brother. He doesn't realize that I must end up with the Singer.

Eventually, it dawns on me that they are so drunk that they won't remember anything in the morning. I push two men out of my front door, one brusquely, one gently.

Then I put David Bowie on the stereo again.

I am drawn to him because I feel unreal. Adrift in a grey city with only faint, thread-like attachments to places and people. I think everyone else feels like this too. The people who dance joyously at parties every evening, the people who daily twist themselves through the ugly tumultuous city, everyone. We are not bound down and any moment now a gust of wind could sweep along the streets and blow us and the city's other rubbish into outer space. Into an empty darkness where we would float around, humans and rubbish, interchangeable.

We are all adrift but he tries to anchor himself. To a place. A run down suburb of the city. I get the train to this suburb. The Singer is waiting for me on the platform. I have no idea what to expect but when I see him I feel his gravitational pull. He takes me straight to the pub from the train station and even though it is only the early afternoon we start getting drunk.

I enter a much smaller world. The Singer reigns over it – around one square mile of hideous suburban city. He rules over it because he loves it so intensely. His family are middle-class, successful, intellectual, but he has rejected this inheritance almost completely. He has changed his surname, changed his accent and disappeared himself – into an anonymous web of suburban streets, into pubs full of men who also do not want to be noticed by the world. Pubs which are more full of bacchanalian, adult joy than anywhere I have been before or since.

I dive headfirst into his world, borrowing his anonymity, hiding myself in a reassuring swarm of men as they shout at football teams projected onto large screens. I swim in masculine bonhomie. I am carefree, elated, addicted.

The Singer is erasing something by being here – not just his name and his accent, but also his past. He hoots and cackles like a thug as he talks with the other men. He fits in perfectly – anyone who wants to drink and laugh and has no need to be admired while he does so fits in here. But the intensity of his attachment to the place makes him burn more brilliantly than the others, so he stands out despite his efforts to efface himself, and not only to me, although I am becoming dazed by my obsession with him. Even the quiet, violent men who have high status here – men who have well-kept, well-dressed women and children and who I sometimes hear talking quietly about guns – recognize and respect his shining love for their territory. I can tell that they see it as something both ridiculous and marvellous.

In retrospect, I think what we saw in him was desperation transformed artfully into joy.

We are lovers for three months before he rejects me.

He lets me join him in his small world, and I curl up contentedly in it, spending as many days in his bed and nights with him at the pub as my work will let me.

I feel at ease in the shabby house that he shares with his brother. The house demands nothing of me. Nobody cleans it, nobody dusts, nobody gardens. The walls are covered in football memorabilia: badges and postcards from his favourite team are shoved into antique mirrors. Once someone tried to make it pretty – feminine friezes are stencilled along the tops of the walls and diseased, unpruned roses ramble in the garden. I cannot imagine trying to feminise this place now. I do not even attempt to leave behind face-cream or a supply of clean underwear. It would be too much of an imposition.

But I feel welcome. The Singer holds me gently as we sleep on his sagging, musty bed in his dusty, badly lit bedroom. It is at the top of the house and is a good place to hide. In the mornings I read in bed while listening to him compose new songs in the spare room on the floor below. I wonder whether the songs are about me but never ask. We eat cheap white bread and watery sausages. He lets me demand sex from him whenever I like. And whenever we have enough money and are not felled by our hangovers we go to the pub.

We take cocaine regularly and I listen to him talk long into the night. One night I take so much cocaine that I find myself leaning on the bar of the pub and talking fluent French to a group of equally wired North African men. I am delighted.

I am completely in love with his world. Such a small pulsating place. So many men to lose myself with, him by my side, as the thighs of football players flash across the screens above our heads and we scream with anger and amazement.

But he is always in a state of tension. He tells me that until recently he has been unable to walk along the street unless he avoided stepping on the cracks between paving stones. He tells me that he is chronically depressed and I know that he is medicated but he doesn't dwell on these things and they seem irrelevant until he rejects me.

It is New Year's Eve. We are in my flat, floating above the centre of the city. It feels very like nowhere after his world.

We spent the week between Christmas and the New Year drinking and taking drugs in Peckham Rye and I feel worn and slightly on edge. During the week things have been difficult between us for the first time. One night I refuse to go to bed with him because I feel slighted by something he has said. I curl up defensively on his sofa, unable to move, silently punishing him for my exhaustion and unease. Eventually he comes down to me:

"Why don't you come to bed?"

I am silent.

"What's the matter?"

Still silent.

"Come to bed, silly."

I force myself to speak though the drugs are weighing heavily in my veins.

"You don't love me"..

"Don't love you?"

"You don't love me enough. You can't."

"Don't be silly. Come to bed."

"I can't."

And really I can't. I am a lead weight pushing down on the broken springs of his sofa. He looks at me quizzically and leaves. An hour later I finally feel my jaw unclench and I climb the three flights of stairs to his room.

But tonight it is New Year's Eve and we are happy. Despite floating in nowhere the Singer flashes with intensity. I watch excitedly as he charms the couple that we have decided to spend the evening with. They are my friends and they fall for him too.

The Singer calls me on the afternoon of January 2. He tells me that he is too mentally fragile to cope with a relationship. With me or anybody else. After the call I go to bed screaming with grief. I am nowhere, so nobody hears me.

The next two months are impossible. I haven't lost a man, I have lost a world. There is nothing that I want to do except dive back into the pool of anonymous men. That is where the light is. Here there is no life or light and their absence is unbearable.

After two months, the grief does not subside, but starts to differentiate. I am able to distinguish between the Singer and his world of men. If I cannot have him, perhaps I can cling on to the world, this perfect-for-me world. I start to send tendrils back into it. I have a drink with the brother, who is gentle and sympathetic. I warm myself on this faint connection. The brother smells my desperation and arranges for me to spend a brief half hour in a pub in the centre of town with both he and the Singer. I am careful to hide what I need from him. To not show any need. I understand that, if I show no need, I may be allowed back into his world. When we meet I deliver an excellent performance of carefree laughter.

After walking away, waving lightly to them, I slam face-first into a lamppost. The impact breaks my nose, but only slightly. For three years afterwards a chip of bone floats just under my left eye.

I take myself back to Peckham Rye, uninvited. I need to feel myself in the heave of drunken men again. I go to his pub, because it is the one I know. Also because he is there, but I think of him as a co-ordinate not a destination. I want the men and their hedonism. Not sexually. Existentially.

But it turns out the Singer is delighted to see me. He spends the evening by my side, carefully weaving me into the conversation of the men who are drinking with us. He admires my muscles, my beauty, calls on the other men to admire me too. I am too drunk, too absorbed by the wonder of being back here to think much. But when his arm slips around my shoulders as we drink and talk wild nonsense to the other men (it is such a relief to be talking it again) it feels natural that it should be there.

It is possible that I try to resist going home with him that night – I do not recall. But I remember the pleasure of being pressed against his soft freckled skin when we get there.

I wake in the middle of the night, as I usually do. The Singer's thunderous snoring stops me falling back to sleep. I take refuge in the small bathroom next to his bedroom and read one of the battered paperback history books that he keeps there. I am too tired to read much, so I stare at the peeling yellow wallpaper, which glares in the fluorescent light. I am restless, as I usually am when I wake in the middle of the night. I want dawn to come, am impatient for another day, for what happens next.

I wander across the small room and stop beside some dusty bamboo shelves. I have looked at them many times before, usually at this time of night. On them is a sort of reliquary of the woman that the Singer used to live with years ago. Pots of face-cream and deodorant are still here, exactly as I imagine she left them. Although at first I was shocked to find them, the fact that they are covered in dust and have never moved is reassuring. The owner of the pots decorated this house many years ago. The yellow wallpaper was her choice, and the floral scrolls which wind around the top of the living room. These should be absurdly feminine in this man's place, but over the years the paper has become tobacco stained and torn and the flowers hardly show through.

As I gaze at the bamboo shelves in my sleepless daze I realize that, though the pots are still dusty and have still not moved, there is a hair-band sitting on the shelf that has never been there before. Exhaustedly, obsessively, I start carefully searching the room for more traces of another woman. Eventually I am successful. I find a used condom in his filthy beer-keg dustbin. It is near the top of the bin, recent, unhidden.

I am revolted. I stay awake for the rest of the night, trapped in the small bathroom by my rage. It is impotent – there is nothing to be done, no justice to be had from this man who has promised me nothing.

It feels like torture, but I stay very close to him a long time after that. I find out who the other woman is and I am often in her company. She has beautiful breasts, paper white skin and drinks even more than I do. I hate him, not her – but don't have the strength not to end up in his bed sometimes though I never feel safe in it again. It is perilous, and I perch in it at the top of the house, waiting to be finally knocked out by a cuckoo.

Then suddenly the way I see him shifts.

He is no longer a magical creature in control of an exotic world of men, a world that I want to nest in. I see now that he is a man terrified of his brain chemistry. His depression is only just kept under control by medication and he constantly walks a tightrope over a black sea that he knows he will fall into, again and again and again.

He senses the shift in my understanding of him and starts to tell me stories about his brokenness. Details his breakdowns, neuroses, paranoia. He instructs me in his madness. I do not think this is to apologize for not being able to love me. I think he is recruiting me. He wants me to put him back together again. My maternal instincts kick in hard. And he is so beautiful.

Music is our medium. Medicine.

The Singer spends all of his days writing his songs but he never performs them because he cannot bear to be looked at. He believes that he is hideous. Photographs of himself traumatize him.

I tell him that I will help him. He is delighted and wary. He lets me know that there are boundaries - that, as with love, there are some things that his madness will not allow him to do. I am calm. From now on I am always calm with him.

When I was very young I rode horses. Young horses that were frightened of everything. They often put me in danger – throwing themselves in front of cars at the sound of pigs screaming in industrial farm buildings, or nearly throwing themselves into plate glass shop-fronts as juggernauts passed us on narrow streets. I learnt to be as calm as a rock, as calm as a tree, to stop the horses killing themselves and me. I was once even calm enough to ride one through a field of burning straw. I use the same technique with the Singer.

Our work together begins. He gives me forty songs to listen to. In each, he is full of a particular kind of longing. For another world in which he and his lover can be whole and free. He sings repeatedly about his brokenness and about going home. The songs are always addressed to a woman who is also broken and needs healing and to go home. They are romantic and domestic. Some were written years ago, for the woman who chose the wallpaper – these are full of regret. Others are more recent and more optimistic. As if he really can imagine escape from the brokenness that crackles beneath his words and voice and harmonies.

For the first twenty times that I listen to each song all I can think about is whether they were written for me. I long for them to have been written for me. Find their sadness acutely erotic.

My obsessive listening allows me to get under the skin of the songs. I learn the tunes and the lyrics immediately, greedily, looking for clues about which woman they have been written for, embroidering meanings that link them to me.

Then I learn the basic architecture of each song – the introduction, verse, chorus – and the middle-eight, when something new comes in just when you think you know everything that the song has to offer. Soon I realize that I know every note, every backing vocal, every drumbeat. When he changes even the smallest element I notice immediately.

He asks me to help him choose the strongest songs. I do so impartially, allow in the songs that belong to other women, as well as those that I can imagine might belong to me. I am surprised that he accepts almost all of my choices. He seems to respect my judgement – though I don't know whether this is just because of he is so relieved to have someone, anyone, to help him wrestle with his work. Only one song he refuses to work further on. Later, his brother tells me this one was written just before his first mental breakdown.

My obsession with him is transferred to his music and we nurture it together. His writing gets better, fed by the blood of my dammed and redirected adoration. We decide to try to create an album of his best songs. He tells me that it will be called *Broken*.

Because he is terrified of performing in public, I throw a party for him in my floating, nowhere flat. I hire the PA system, set it up, rehearse him. His unease makes him aggressive. I stay calm.

He cannot drink until he performs, and cannot perform until his best friend, the Woodsman, arrives. The Woodsman does not arrive until 10pm by which time the Singer is almost despairing. His set is very weak, and he sidles and apologises between each song. But the audience of friends that we have gathered are kind.

It is a relief when it is over and we all get drunk and dance wild dances in the dark. Drip wax over my rented furniture and stick feathers in our hair. Somebody wears my stuffed fox-brush as a tail, falls over backwards and breaks the tail's spine.

Some of the Singer's friends from out of town are there and though I hardly know them I offer to let them sleep in my bed. The Singer and I also need somewhere to sleep so we share a single bed in my small spare room. We do not kiss but he wraps his arm around my waist. I am so drunk that as we lie together I whisper under my breath, not intending him to hear:

"I adore you."

"I know you do," he replies. His tone of voice is matter of fact. There is nothing warm in it.

As we start to work on his music together, I sometimes still kid myself that there is something romantic and loving between us. Though I am perched and perilous, I still dream of a future where we will be whole and happy, the future that he promises to the woman he sings to in his songs. We still sometimes end up in bed together. Still sometimes fuck. But as I become more important to his music, he withdraws further from me sexually and I know he is seeing more and more of the other woman. I think that he does not want to owe me too much.

I can no longer enjoy being in the pub with the men. The pain is too strong. Being there with the other woman, who drinks more than me, is wilder than me, more native. She has rich black hair, porcelain skin and beautiful breasts that the Singer admires, as he used to admire me. I do not know yet that she will suffer even more than I have. But my connection with him now is stronger than ever. I am shaping his work, directing his days, managing his moods. And even without romance or sex our connection sustains and thrills me. It becomes the focus of my days.

It is my birthday. The Singer arrives at my flat with four new songs. I told him to write new songs for the album and he has followed my instructions. This makes me feel powerful. But he tells me that he is not going to come out and drink with my friends this evening or stay with me tonight, even though it is my birthday.

We play the songs in my big empty nowhere flat. They are the best he has written. He tells me that the second song is my song, and he is giving it to me as my birthday present.

And your arms will save me
And your pain will save me
What you lose will save me

Something shifts again in me. It is as if the song has fulfilled me, closed a circle. Or perhaps that it has brought the deal that we have made tacitly (my pain for his salvation) too far into the light. I tell him that I never want to fuck him again.

For the first and last time on that evening of my birthday we have a lucid conversation about our relationship. He tells me that all his friends tell him that he should marry me. I tell him that his infidelity is unbearable, and that anyhow I think that he is right to say that he is too mad to sustain a relationship with anyone.

And then it is over.

Later, he will claim that it never happened.

The aftershock of the affair shapes my life for a long time. For a long time I can only imagine happiness in the form that the Singer, and his songs, and his pubs and the men in them have shown me. And his need for me is magnetic. We continue to work together on *Broken*, smoothing and intensifying the songs. I don't believe that he ever wrote better ones than the ones he wrote under my direction.

I coach his live performances, mouthing the words to every song as he sings it, shouting them out from the side of the stage when he forgets them, utterly bound up in every performance as if it was I myself on stage (though I have no desire to perform). He slowly becomes as charming in on stage as he is in a pub. I am fiercely proud of every performance.

He becomes restless, so I tell him that I am taking him away. One searingly hot August, I take him to Sicily and Rome. Holidays have been impossible for him, but by this time we know each other well enough to know that he will survive, protected by the steady calm that I can generate because he needs it.

This is the real end of our affair. He sits in the window of our cheap pension in Palermo and sings a new song that he has written about the other woman and I long for him and feel the absurdity of how close we are. Each night we get drunk together and I long for him and only the gap between two uncomfortable single beds separates us. In Rome, we find a basement dive with a little stage and each night he sits on a stool and nervously sings covers. And each night I sit by the stage in a group of tourists, men and women who are always there, and I see him radiate his crackling mad beautiful light and I long.

Each night he sings: *"Did I disappoint you?*

Leave a bad taste in your mouth?"

And I drunkenly mouth Yes, Yes, Yes.

But I never do anything about my longing. This is the arrangement. I am allowed to be this close to him – close enough to hear him breathe, to sense his desire for other women, to know when he is wrestling with his madness and when he is at peace – as long as I don't take a step closer. But even so it leaks out somehow, this absurd, thrumming longing.

One afternoon, we are walking off our hangovers through a dusty Roman suburb and he becomes suddenly uneasy.

"What are we doing here?"

"What do you mean?"

"Why did you bring me here?"

"You needed a break. A holiday. You said you needed a break."

He laughs.

"Is that why we're here?"

"Yes. Of course."

"But why are you here?"

"I'm your manager. I'm here because you

needed a holiday."

"What the fuck are we doing here, though? What are you trying to trick me into?"

"Nothing."

"You want me, don't you?"

"No, no, of course not."

"But you're beautiful. Why aren't you on holiday with someone who wants you?"

"I can do that another time."

He laughs sceptically.

We go to St Peter's. As we walk out of the harsh sunlight into its enormous gloom, I am overwhelmed and can't breathe.

I walk away from him into the heart of the cathedral, as it soars around me. I turn to my right where there is a small chapel. Walking out of the vastness into the chapel I am enfolded. Women in black are praying to a picture. I sit down among them and start sobbing.

The women think I am in mourning and put their arms around me.

Noel

I'm sitting in the middle of a rubbish-strewn inner-city square on a summer's evening. There is a man with me. We have been lovers for a while, but I am becoming sick of his desire to mend me. I think he really wants me to be insane, incapable, desperate. And I am not.

I'm bored of him and his concern for my wellbeing, so I look around the square at the other drinkers. We are in a part of town that has become suddenly fashionable. Everyone here wears edgy clothes, their hair sculpted architecturally, their faces blank, waiting to be looked at. Except for one young man who sits under the square's only tree wearing a cheap tracksuit. Like me, he is watching the crowd, but with more intent. He catches my eye and I look away.

Moments later the young man appears beside us.

"Do you by any chance have a light?" he asks.

The boy is smoking a butt-end. He tells us that he wouldn't usually smoke a butt-end, but that things have gone wrong for him today. My lover commiserates with him briefly and tries to end the conversation, but the boy stays. He wants to tell us his story. He tells us that his girlfriend has beaten him up and kicked him out.

"Can you see the fucking black eye she's given me?"

We can see no bruising, although his pupils look unusually large, as if he is in some darkness that we do not share.

"But it's not me that I'm worried about. I don't care about me and I don't care about her. But Jakey." There is a genuine catch in his voice. He hides it by taking a long drag of his cigarette butt.

"I've known him since he was six months old. She's too off her face most of the time to look after him. I feel like I want to break down her door just to make sure he's had his breakfast."

I expect the story to go on and on and that we will have sympathy and cash wrung out of us. But the boy stops himself and gives a genuine and gentle apology for disturbing our summer's evening. He chats about less troubling things. Is charming. After a few minutes I offer to buy him a drink.

"That's very kind of you. Buying a drink for a stranger. I can't return the favour I'm afraid."

I tell him not to worry, and give him twenty pounds. As he walks off across the square to the bar, my lover raises an eyebrow at me. I tell him that I like the boy, believe him. That there is something about him that I find compelling. An innocence.

Strangely the man that loves to heal broken things doesn't appear to understand.

My phone rings.

"Hello... it's Noel. You gave me your number the other night. Do you remember?"

"Of course I do."

"How are you?"

"Fine thanks."

"And how's your boyfriend?"

"I don't know."

"I thought he was a lovely bloke."

"I find him a bit soft." I laugh, and so does Noel. Then after the laughter, silence.

"I'm calling because I'm a bit desperate. She won't let me back in, or give me any of my stuff. I've been sleeping on a bench since I met you."

I'm pleased that he has called me. It makes me feel necessary. I think this will be an uncomplicated transaction. I have found a baby bird with its beak gaping wide. All I need to do is stuff in food.

I go back to the square to see him. It is deserted now, except for Noel who sits on the only bench carefully poised with his feet square on the ground. He jerks up at the sight of me.

"I didn't think you'd come."

"Why not?"

"I don't know. I've learnt not to expect much from people."

We wander around the city for an hour. I find that I am enjoying myself, that it is easy to talk to him about simple things. And once again I am struck by his gentleness. There is something alive in him that I expected to be dead: he stops and talks to the dogs that we meet as we walk; wants to feed the drab city birds; wants to know about me. I tell him very little about myself, but I get the impression that he is memorizing everything that I say. He asks me for nothing but, before I leave, I give him money, hope that he'll spend it on food.

I have had enough of my boyfriend. I tell him that his desire to mend me is freaking me out, that I think that he himself is so weak that he needs his lovers to be broken so that he can feel powerful while trying to mend them. I do not tell him that he is a disappointing lover, although this also is true.

Our last morning together is awkward. His enormous eyes are damp with tears, his soft flesh clammy. I cannot wait to walk away from the mess in his room, the confusion on his face.

I have time on my hands, so when Noel calls me again I suggest that he comes to meet me at my favourite pub. It turns out that he is an excellent drinking partner.

We start to meet about once a week. I never call Noel, but he soon works out how often he can call me without pissing me off. If I don't feel like seeing him I just tell him to call back in a few days.

I know that he would like to cling to me, wishes that I could transform his life with a wave of my wand. I plan to allow him close enough to warm himself on our connection, but I don't want him to get too comfy.

Noel and I like to get very drunk together. We always drink at the same pub in the centre of the city. Noel drinks cider, and I drink vodka and soda, the only drink that my stomach, which is weak, can tolerate.

One night, we start talking to a man who is sitting beside us at the bar. He has the cardboard tag from a prestigious horse race threaded through his button-hole, and an enormous duffel bag on the floor beside his bar-stool. He tells us that he is the racing correspondent for a newspaper. Tells us a convoluted story about his day. We ask him what is in the bag and he opens it for us. It is full of cash, heavy with bills and coins.

We like to go to an American diner after the pub. This is the only food I can get Noel to eat. He likes chips with gravy on them, but is seldom hungry. I force him to eat, knowing that when he is not with me he has other priorities.

Sometimes, at the end of the night, he asks me

for money. Sometimes I give it to him.

We get drunk and talk. When we are only a little drunk, we talk about the present.

When we first start drinking together, he is sleeping on the streets and begging. He knows he doesn't have to do this, and eventually he manages to pull together the documentation he needs to get help from the social services. They get him a place at a hostel. It is full of other addicts and he hates it.

We talk about his lovers. A career woman picks him up on a bus, takes him to her house, feeds and fucks him. She wants to keep him. He is very flattered and enlivened by this, but decides that he needs to be free in order to sort himself out. Another street-sleeper, a beautiful girl with long black hair and tattoos becomes obsessed with him. They sleep together in doorways for a few weeks, but he leaves her. He thinks she is too weak to survive. He has an addict's skinny wiriness, large fine eyes, freckles. I can see why the women want him, even though he is nothing, has nothing.

He is not sentimental about these women. His sentimentalism is reserved for the boy, Jakey, and for me.

And then we talk about the past. These stories gradually drip out, at our most drunken moments. I cannot tell what is true, what elaborated. It is all almost absurdly painful. I do not mind listening. I am almost turned on by the awfulness.

These stories. True or false they come bubbling up.

A stepfather endlessly beats Noel and his sisters. Keeps them locked in a dark cupboard for years, until Noel, finally grown into a teenager with muscles and fury of his own, fights back. He escapes but he cannot live with the thought of his sisters still in pain, still in the darkness. So he goes back, bides his time, until he is able to finish it all.

That is all that Noel says at the end of that story, that he finished it. Then he lapses into silence. I ask him what he means, but he refuses to tell me. I am sure that he wants me to think that he killed the man. Perhaps he did. Or perhaps he just needs to believe that he did, and needs me to bear some kind of partial witness to the imaginary murder. I stop probing him. He doesn't want me to know. I don't want to know.

After that is finished, he finishes it, Noel leaves home and falls on his feet. A woman changes everything. A girlfriend whom he adores. They live together in a council flat. She becomes pregnant and he thinks his life is full of light and hope. They share the care of the infant between them, neither of them works so they just spend their time loving the child and each other. Then one day, while Noel is taking care of him, the baby dies unexplainably. The girl cannot forgive him for letting this happen. Her grief makes her turn him out of the flat.

I am sure that this story is true, although the one element I am not certain of is whether the baby just died, or whether Noel had some hand in her dying. Something careless, not deliberate, the sort of thing you would work very hard to try and forget.

After this, he is destitute for the first time, and for some reason makes his way to a university town. Joins the large community of homeless people that roam the streets there. I wonder if he ever notices the delicate and ancient beauty that surrounded him. He never mentions it. But he is introduced to another beauty that quickly dominates his days and nights. It is not hard for a boy with pretty eyes to beg enough to feed his habit from the river of tourists that runs through the elegant streets.

He finds a friend. An elderly academic, who lives and works in one of the beautiful colleges. Noel strikes up a conversation with him, as he did with me, and the old man becomes his first disinterested benefactor - though am I disinterested? Was the old man? Did he not perhaps just want a pretty boy in his chambers? The academic comforts Noel in his grief and sees some spark of life in him, despite the drugs. He gives him books to read, feeds him occasionally. He tells Noel that he has the potential to grow into something strong and good. Noel feels that he might be right.

But before Noel has learnt enough to even contemplate reading the books the old man dies. Of course he does. And Noel hits the streets even harder.

Listening to these stories gives me some sort of strange relief.

I can always tell when Noel has been taking smack. He is vague, less funny, and his irises are lost in the darkness of his pupils. Eventually I tell him that I won't drink with him anymore unless he goes into rehab. His social worker gets him a place somewhere. He calls me a week into his treatment, the first time he is allowed to use a phone. He sounds exhausted.

"I hate it here."

"Why?"

"I feel like I'm a rat in a cage."

"I'm sorry."

"I don't care enough about myself to go through this. I only came here because you wanted me to."

Three days later, he leaves the programme. I am furious with him and he goes into hiding for a few weeks. But it is boring without him, and I am glad when he calls again. We go out and get drunk.

I am flying off to a tropical island at the other side of the planet, to an international negotiation that everyone knows will fail. I am helping to plan for this failure. Trying to make something grow out of its ruins. Being so far away, so jetlagged, is only made bearable by an old Finn who, when he is drunk, sings songs about how he will hunt the bear, kill the bear, eat the bear and then drink wine from the bear's skull.

The Finn is a wily negotiator, and I depend on his advice and his soft old skin (it always strikes me how old men have the softest skin) to survive in this strange environment – humans thrown together from all parts of the globe to take part in the grandiose, helpless formal dance of diplomacy in air-conditioned hotels on idyllic beaches.

I will be away for weeks, and it seems absurd to leave my nowhere flat empty when Noel is still in his hostel. He always tells me that having nowhere proper to live is what stops him from getting better. So I fill the cupboards with the kind of food I think that he might eat. Leave him with the keys and a set of ground rules. Visitors not allowed. He promises he will adhere to my rules, and I believe him.

He is excited at the thought of this piece of normality, although still gloomy about what will happen to him afterwards. I don't know how to alleviate his gloom, but have a vague hope that something in him will shift when he is in this safe space.

When I return three weeks later, awry with jetlag, I find shit and vomit smeared on the walls of my bedroom. My sheets and mattress are stained, my bathroom a morass. But nothing has been stolen. Nothing broken.

In the few weeks after he fouls my flat, Noel calls me constantly. I don't answer so he leaves messages. Some are miserable and apologetic, some defensive and full of excuses. I continue to ignore his calls and eventually they die away. I still wonder what he is doing, whether he has found some way to grow up out of the shit, but I don't want to talk to him. I want to punish him for his failure to function like a normal human being.

Then there is a year of silence during which the smell evaporates from the flat, and the stains bleach away. I wonder about him, but I don't call.

Sixteen months in Noel starts calling me again. He leaves excited messages, insisting on seeing me. In the messages he tells me that he has changed, that he wants me to meet the new him. I agree. I am curious.

When we meet again, I barely recognize him as he has put on so much weight. All muscle. His neck is revoltingly thick, his face swollen with good health, arms and legs slabs of meat. He is terribly proud of this new body. Tells me that what he did to my flat made him want to change. That he got himself clean with no help from the medical profession. Just found somewhere to suffer alone. I don't know whether to believe him, but his pupils are no longer lost in the dark.

He is working for a family of gypsies fifty miles away from the city. He says they are very rich. They make their money from building work, make huge profits by ignoring safety regulations, sending Noel and others up onto roofs without scaffolding or rope. The gypsies own a large house, but all live together in a few downstairs rooms, cannot bear to inhabit their house like ordinary, sedentary folk. They let Noel live in an old, unheated caravan in the garden of the house. He loves their dogs and is learning to course rabbits.

He still doesn't have any money. The gypsies pay him in food, beer, cigarettes and lodging. I tell him that it sounds as if he is their slave. This doesn't register.

We become close again. I want to reward him for his good behaviour, encourage him to stay fat and strong. And I am increasingly alone – drifting away from my family and friends, with whom I seem to have very pointless relationships. The happy ones don't need me, for they are happy anyhow. And the miserable ones are all stuck in their misery, circling around and around it, taking bites out of their own tails then wondering why are in pain. I am no use to them.

But Noel seems to offer hope. He might be capable of making the transition from dark to light.

Once a month, Noel asks the gypsies for enough money to come up to London for the weekend to see me. They usually only give him enough for a one-way fare. I pay for the return trip.

We go back to our pub, get drunk, eat at the diner. When we get home I make him a bed on the sofa in my flat but he never sleeps. Instead, he plays music to himself endlessly on my stereo – two of my albums on a repeat loop. On one, a woman sings mournfully about the loss of love. On the other, a vicious rapper taunts his girlfriend with violent threats. When I wake in the night to go to the toilet, Noel is crouching on my green leather sofa, slowly drinking a can of cider and smoking a roll-up. I have bought myself a white rabbit, and sometimes when I look in on them I see she is sitting on his lap, sharing in his all-night vigil.

When I wake like this I always suggest that he gets some sleep, and he always says that he will. But when I get up in the morning, the music is still playing, and he is still perched and alert, ready to go out and buy me whatever I want for breakfast.

I find these all night music sessions intensely irritating. But I am glad to have him, safe and almost whole, under my roof.

This year we have Christmas together. I cannot face my mother, am suspended in space. I cannot pretend to be warm and present. And I know that I can make Noel happy. I fill him a stocking full of nonsense, cook turkey, make fake gravy and other things that I think he might eat. It is a strangely mild winter and we have our Christmas dinner on the balcony of my flat. After we have eaten, we walk two miles through the deserted streets to visit a transvestite who is getting stoned with a beautiful woman who used to be the lover of some famous but over-the-hill international tennis player. They are watching trashy Christmas TV together. The room is silent except for the TV blaring.

Noel smokes with them then spends the evening happily staring at the woman's breasts.

In the New Year, I start to find Noel's dependence on me suffocating. I stop answering his calls.

Rich Boy

Right in the centre of the city, close to my nowhere flat, an exquisite old house has money poured over it. The money washes away the dreary institutional fixtures and fittings of the sensible charity that used to live in the house and in their place blossom exotic wallpapers, delicate gold footed sofas, velvety carpets soft enough to lie naked on, harpsichords painted with violets and roses, white plaster reliefs of cornucopias, fat women and bulls balls set against eau de nil walls, vitrines full of perilously fragile porcelain, mirrored bars lined with endless bottles of unheard of liqueurs.

It is as if the house (which was originally like this, was built for wildly extravagant parties and impossibly beautiful intrigues) has been asleep for a couple of centuries and the river of money wakes it up with a start, like a prince's kiss.

I am a member of this club. I cannot resist its opulence, the intricate silver laid out on white linens, the tassels of its cushions, the servility of the uniformed staff, the heat of the sauna that lurks like a dragon in its basement, the sweet smelling lotions that masseurs rub into my skin after a long day doing my virtuous, futile work. I like to invite earnest colleagues here to discuss serious things, I buy them tea – pretty tricky things served on turrets of china and silver – and they blink and stutter in amazement.

But the best thing about the club is its parties. I go to one with a man I barely know, someone I have met over cocktails the night before, who I told about the club and who was enchanted just by my stories of it and demanded to come. I am not attracted to him, but we go with a beautiful couple, a very young, sweet, peach-skinned girl and her dark lover, a man who has occasionally also been my lover and who I think I would like to love properly, though I have given up on him after many fractured attempts at making closer contact.

But this is irrelevant now as the bright light of a party at the beautiful house is shining on us.

The house was built in the eighteenth century and, for this party, we have been instructed to dress as its first inhabitants would have for their wildest parties: masked and dressed as aristocracy. So the peach-skinned girl and I spend an afternoon burrowing through rows and rows of hooped petticoats and vicious corsets on the fourth floor of a costumier in the theatre district of the city.

We choose extraordinary dresses from a myriad display of silks and taffetas, hers apricot and mine pale green, soft collapsing carapaces that are deceptively deflated as they hang on rails high above us. Before we are allowed to try them on, we are brought layers and layers of undergarments, piles of muslin, soft cotton bloomers and loosely laced petticoats and strange cotton stockings that protect us from the dresses, and the dresses from us.

Over these layers go the corsets, which terrify us as we cannot imagine being able to breathe in them and then over the corsets go the hoops, which are not really hoops but huge oval cages covered in more white muslin and fastened with ribbons around the tiny waists that we have suddenly obtained thanks to the corsets.

And then finally, over all this, the costumier's assistants lower our dresses and pull more ribbons and we turn to the mirrors and see that we have become new creatures, vastly wide-hipped, tiny-waisted, plump-breasted creatures. We laugh and feel that we could sweep the world up in our skirts and carry it away with us.

And so we take these new creatures, ourselves but narrower, wider, far more splendid, to the party and our escorts wear tricorned hats and velvet breeches and shirts with frothy necks and we climb carefully out of the taxi (we can't quite believe that we have both fitted into the taxi, we are so wide) and out into a warm still city night. Outside the club huge torches have been lit and send orange flames into the sky.

We sweep up the steps through the flames and double doors are opened for us and we sweep onwards, over chequered floor tiles and past painted panels and as we sweep we are handed fragile glasses of champagne and we feel from behind our masks the murmur of approval from the rooms we sweep through.

To begin with, we simply move through the rooms, which are arranged in circles around the circular stairwell, revelling in this new sense of being vast ships that make rooms flutter in their wakes, round and around through the rooms on

one floor we sweep, then round and round again
and up the staircase, watched by neoclassical busts
set against fake marbling – and then through the
more delicate rooms on the higher floor, round
and around, and as we move we flap our fans and
practice flying them open and snapping them shut
in time to our steps.

And, as we walk, we feel as though we are
sewing ourselves into the house, as though our
dresses and therefore ourselves are part of its
fabric, as though the house's old soul has woken
up and decided to come and dance amongst our
vast skirts.

But, after a while, we start to tire a little of our
progress and so we stop and sink onto a silk sofa,
and our men -who have been following us with
bemused, indulgent smiles - go to fetch more
champagne. Then we start to watch the other
people in their silks and velvets, and we are
pleased with what we see, and feel that the house
is too, for everyone is as magnificent as we are.
And we wonder about the faces that are hidden
behind masks, and ask one another whether
everyone could really be as beautiful as the little
pieces of face that they are revealing suggest.

And then the men return and we drink more, and then start to feel restless and want to dance, but our corsets are so tight that we are not sure if we will be able to. We think that perhaps cocaine will help us forget the corsets so we all skitter up another more private flight of stairs to an elegant little bathroom and we sniff it up and then skitter back down, down, down to the grand room at the bottom of the staircase where suddenly everyone is dancing, and then we find that dancing is the real point of our dresses, dancing with masks that liberate us and fans that give us power, silks and velvets whirring in circles, diagonals, fractal patterns, weaving in and out of one another in the heart of the old house.

And then suddenly there is no-one left on the dance floor except a thin man in black velvet breeches and a black silk mask, and I am across from him on the other side of the room, and, for the first time, I notice the polished floor that we have been dancing across, with its herringbone of old wood seeming to set out the steps of the dances that we have been dancing, the old house orchestrating our dance.

And the thin man reaches out to me across the

herringbone and I slap my fan in the air at him, and then the real dance begins.

I have never danced like this, my gliding skirts, my gloved arms, the flash of my fan in the air. The thin man leaps at my side, following the patterns that I create, that coalesce in me as the dress and the drug and the old house arch my back, rack my neck, send me whirling (but I am powerful, controlled, elegant) around the room. He is light, wonderfully light, light and responsive, and he understands the patterns, understands the beauty that is being woven through me, through us, and he husbands it, catches it lightly then flings it out into the air again, flings me and the beauty into the air but we land softly and so the patterns can unfurl again, again and again and again.

Nobody else puts a foot on the dance floor as we dance. But I can feel them watching us, and their watching is a part of the dance, they are standing in a line that reaches around us and watching, and behind them the walls and windows are watching too, and their stillness is also a part of the dance, the bone of the dance against which the muscles push, the ribs of the dance within which the lungs heave, the heart of the dance through which the blood rushes and rushes and rushes.

And then it is over. He flings me into the air a last time, and I sink a billow of silk into his arms and we are still and we know that this time the stillness is not part of the dance, but its end. And his eyes look at me through the almond shaped slits in his mask and his mouth grins and I know that there is no sex between us, only the dance. So I drop lower into my skirts, into a curtsy, and he bows deeply and then I walk off the floor, over the herringbone patterns, in one direction, and he walks away in the other.

A while later, I am standing alone, leaning against one of the old walls, and a masked girl comes up to me and tells me: he is a famous dancer you know, he dances for the Royal Ballet, you should be very proud that he danced with you like that.

But that is not how life is normally. Normally things are smaller, more prosaic, and I am not able to wear skirts that are as nearly wide as I am tall. Though for a long while after that party, I grieve for them and wish desperately that I could.

I also wish desperately that life could be studded with parties like that, parties that lift you into the air and let you hover in the way in which you hover above the room, above your friends, your family, your dreary limited life while everyone gasps in amazement in those extraordinary dreams in which you can fly.

But I cannot see how there could be more parties like that, so I grieve. And when it is my birthday I have a very small quiet party in the old house, hoping that an echo, a ghost of the other party will ring through it.

My little party is in a small anteroom that leads off the procession of elegant drawing rooms on the first floor of the club. The anteroom is painted in the palest eau-de-nil, against which white plaster mouldings of fruit and flowers twirl. The room is small and the walls are lined with vitrines made of carved wood and polished glass and filled with delicate porcelain things – teapots and vases and ladies with their hair piled impossibly high and skirts as wide as the skirts that I dream of – so that the room feels crowded with glass and carved spindly wooden legs and porcelain fantasy and sitting on a sofa in the middle of the room I feel as though I too am one of the exhibits, but cruder.

Only a handful of people come to the party. They trickle into the little room, perch on the small silk sofas, sip champagne, talk animatedly about nothing much. It all seems trivial and the ghosts of the masked party only emphasise how dowdy we are in our modern clothes, how dowdy and scruffy and dark. Early in the evening an old friend draws me to one side and tells me that she is pregnant. She is the first of my really close friends to become pregnant and this seems to be the only important thing that is going to happen in the little room that night.

A new, noisy, blonde friend arrives late with a small man whom I have never met. I am not quite sure why the blonde and I have become friends. We met at a very formal conference – she is a rather tabloid academic who has been writing about the protests against globalization and I do not respect her. She seems to be surfing a wave of interest in such matters without really seeking to understand what it actually takes (clarity, strategy, an understanding of the system, I think) to change the world. But she seems interested in me, in my life and my work, and she seems to respect my opinions, so I like being with her. And it feels good to have someone slightly notorious at my party. She introduces me to the little man that she has brought with her – they are old family friends, both Jewish and from the North of the city where so many of the clever, intricately networked Jews live.

The little man seems pleased to meet me, and talks enthusiastically about the old house, which pleases me. When I move away and talk to my few other guests, I am aware that he has fallen silent, and think that he is watching me and listening to my conversation.

But nothing else happens at the party so I am disappointed and lie back on the sofa and close my eyes and imagine myself in the wide skirts again. When my guests start to dwindle (having drunk as much champagne as they are able to bear at an occasion where there is no dancing and no obvious opportunity for random seduction) I start to feel quite bleak.

The little man comes up to me. He wears thick black glasses, and pushes them up his nose before he speaks.

"You look glum."

"I am glum. It's all over, but nothing's happened yet."

"Well, let's go and make something happen then."

I eye him sceptically. He doesn't seem to have the glamour that I'm looking for.

"Come on. I've got a new car. I'll drive you somewhere in it."

I have nothing else to look forward to except my empty nowhere flat, still stained from Noel's soiling, so reluctantly I agree. I am so uninterested in the little man that I let him see my reluctance. It doesn't seem to put him off.

His car is a tiny, souped-up version of a classic tiny car. Inside it is stripped of all the usual paddings and panellings so that it feels like a cold bare skeleton. He tells me that it has a huge engine, and he drives it murderously fast through the dark city. I am quite frightened and also irritated as it has terrible suspension and I am bounced violently by every pothole and speed-bump.

I ask him where we are going.

He says: "I don't know. But before I take you

there, I want to show you something."

He drives me north to the most beautiful of the city's formal parks, and then drives me along one of the fine roads strung along the park's edges. To our right stretches out a procession of extraordinarily grand white-pillared villas, while to our left the park sleeps, densely dark, so dark that the archaic street lamps seem about to be swallowed by it.

It is the darkest place in the city, and beautiful. I have always longed to live here. But he is driving so fast that I think perhaps I might die here instead, tonight.

At the end of the procession of white fantasies he slams on the breaks and stops outside an even more wonderful, much older vast red brick house in a courtyard with beautiful trees and a chapel. We sit in silence for a moment and I enjoy the feeling of stillness and not being dead yet. And then I start to breathe again, and I enjoy resting my eyes on the old brick, which is lit gently against the overwhelming dark that looms from the park.

"I'm thinking of buying this house," he says out of the darkness.

I laugh.

"No, I really am thinking of buying it. Would you like to live here, beautiful girl?"

I would. But I cannot imagine living here with this little man, so I laugh again, nervously this time.

We get back into the car in silence and then he swings the car around in a circle on the dark road and shoots it back into the heart of the city. He seems carefree and jolly as he slams through the gears and stamps on the accelerator. Between jolts of terror, at junctions, corners, straight stretches of road, zebra crossings, traffic lights, I try to digest the thought of his wealth.

The little car screams to a halt before I have had the chance to. We are back in the messy, tawdry centre, my territory, on a back street a few blocks from my flat. I wonder why we are here. There is nothing here except the stink from rubbish from a street market, rotting fruit, fish blood, old cabbage.

"Come on, beautiful," he says, still sounding intensely jolly despite the stench and the ugly street-lit darkness and the lateness of the night, and swings himself neatly out of the car. I crawl out after him, and suddenly feel an ache of exhaustion. It is well into the early hours, and I am still not sure why I am here.

The little man trots up some steps to a black door with an opaque circular window in it. I linger on the street, not sure if I want to follow him.

He grins down at me. "Come on beautiful girl. You'll like it here."

Here is incredibly dark. Even after the dark streets walking into the place feels like going blind. An elegant woman with ferociously dark lipstick is sitting behind a small desk near the door. The only light comes from a single white candle in a tall silver candlestick that sits on her desk. Her face is white in the candlelight and her hair, cut into an impossibly straight fringe, seems to be dyed purple. But I can't tell for sure in the dark.

She greets the little man courteously and invites him to sign a large black leather bound book. When he has done so she leaps up and takes his coat, then disappears with it into the darkness and comes back a moment later, stroking her strange, shining hair. She doesn't look at me or acknowledge that I'm here, but asks him to follow her down a narrow, pitch-dark corridor.

He turns and grins again. "Come on. Let me buy you a drink."

I follow him through the dark, and suddenly we find ourselves in a tiny room lit by another single candle. There is nothing in the room except a small table and two black leather stools. The purple haired woman slips quietly away and we are all alone, although the walls of the room do not reach the ceiling and I can hear quiet murmurings coming from beyond them.

The small, grinning man invites me to sit down, and I do.

"I brought you here because I can tell you like the dark."

"I'm surprised that we got here alive." I say. "But perhaps we're not alive. It's hard to tell in here."

"Don't mind my driving. It's my only rebellion. Otherwise I am a very good boy."

I raise an eyebrow at him through the gloom.

"Let's have a strong cocktail and celebrate the butt-end of your birthday."

I do like the dark. It feels very soothing, not knowing whether one's eyes are open or closed.

And the cocktail, when it arrives, is a milky, powerful thing that glows in the candlelight and numbs me so that I feel I really might be dreaming.

"So," I murmur at him across the darkness, my tongue feeling thick with vodka and exhaustion. "What does it feel like to be so very rich?"

"It's a nightmare," he says, and laughs, and for the first time I hear nervousness in his voice. "I can do anything I choose to in the world and no-one will ever take me seriously."

Half asleep in the darkness I start to feel sorry for him.

The little man and I become friends. I know he is courting me and he knows that I am not interested. He knows because I shake him off at the end of this and every other subsequent evening. And because I tell him so. I am harsh with him because it is easy to be, because he pants after me like a little dog. A burly little terrier tough enough to stay enthusiastic even after you kick it.

I kick him regularly, but I like him. I like him because he likes me and tells me that I am magnificent. And I like his extraordinary amount of restless energy. It is as if his wealth propels him forward ceaselessly, forces him to continually take action although he doesn't appear to have any clear plan about what to do with himself. But he wants to do something significant. Something beautiful. Something that will show he has value beyond the money. He has decided that this something should be making movies, telling stories, creating magic.

He has taken courses and rented offices and hired assistants to help him do this and he flings himself around the city from meeting to meeting, continually racking up parking tickets that the assistants spend much of their time paying, always late and always distracted, as if he is continually listening to some inner voice that screams at him to move faster, do more, be more extreme. I think that he must think that he will sink, evaporate, disintegrate, if he stops.

He calls me continually. I become part of his project. I am a sounding board, a muse, someone to drag along in his wake. I don't mind. It's a fun ride. But I don't think much of his stories.

How am I? I am exhausted. I travel. I am doing

work that terrifies me. I am glad to be swept up and driven off across the city at mad speeds. I am too busy to take anything seriously.

When I stop working I just want to get drunk, and the little man is happy to get drunk with me. I work until late at night, when his merry-go-round of a day has started to slow down, finally, so that when I call him, looking for distraction, he is often available. If I call too early I am rebuffed by a diary of appointments that cover his days like armour.

When we meet, it is often so late that even his drinking club is closed, so we end up at his apartment, which is on the first floor of a fine terraced house in the north of the city. The apartment mostly consists of one vast room with towering ceilings and huge sash windows that are about twice the little man's height. The apartment's other rooms are tucked behind the vast room in what once must have been corridors and cupboards. One room is so narrow that it is basically no more than a blind corridor with a door at one end.

But the big room is a fine one – although per-petually cluttered by a mess of technology and strange art which even the Filipino maid, who his mother sends over to him every morning, doesn't seem able to tame. The windows rise above this mess, looking out on handsome trees in an elegant park that starts just opposite the flat. The few times that I am there in daylight the windows are so large that it seems that the trees might decide to climb through them and join in the conversation about stories and cameras and art. But I think they might be bored.

At night, all you can really see through the windows are a few pearls of brilliant white light coming from the ornate streetlamps that line the walkways in the park. This soothes me and I stare out at them as he paces and talks at me.

Usually, he tries out his stories on me. "This one is about a Filipino maid going home to the Philippines for the first time after working for the same family in England for twenty years. Her employers love her, but they take her for granted and she is always very humble and quiet around them. And socially of course she is the lowest of the low. But back in the Philippines, where she has been funding her extended family for years, she is treated like, no – she *is,* a queen. Because, you see, she is the boss of the family – more powerful than the men, and of course than all the other women, except perhaps for one old bird who also used to work in London. And even though for years she has known this would happen, and has looked forward to it, it takes her a while to get used to being queen, and when she does start to get used to it she also realises that all this politics goes with it – the resentment of the men, the envy of the women. And she hates it so much that, in the end, she has a heart to heart with the old bird and tells her that she is going home. To England. And the old bird just nods her head sagely and says nothing.

"But of course when she gets back to England things are difficult for her again, because now she is no longer the queen, just the little cleaning slave. So the film ends with her being unhappy everywhere."

As I listen, I think that there is something rather unsavoury about writing stories about his servants, and that the idea that servitude might be a happier state than power is particularly dodgy. But being unhappy everywhere seems to me like a good theme for a film, and I tell him so. And then he gets very excited, because I am usually rude about his stories, and he paces more and tells me about other ideas that are less good, and I wish that he would focus on just one thing, and as I am wishing this and also half wishing that I was at home in bed, he leaps up and says I must show you this thing, this thing that I have bought, and he comes over and leaps up and down some more, right in front of the big soft chair that I am sitting in, until I realise that he wants me to get up and follow him.

So I do, regretfully, because the chair is big and soft and I am so nearly drifting to sleep. And he trots off down the little corridor at the back of the big room, which leads into the slightly bigger corridor that is his spare bedroom, and - although I expect him to - he doesn't turn the light on. The only light that comes into the corridor room is from a distant streetlamp in a road that runs past the end of the garden. And this pale, ugly artificial light catches on a glass case that I now see fills the end of the corridor room, a glass case with a gold metal frame, but it is so dark that I cannot see what is in the case.

"Go in," the little man says from behind me. "Go in and look at her."

So I go further in, until I am about a metre away from the glass case and, when I am this close, I can see what is in it and I nearly scream. But I don't, and instead laugh with delight, because of the surprise in the darkness and because she is so pretty.

In the case, a small girl, about seven years old, stands patiently looking at me in the darkness. She is an absolutely real little girl, wearing real clothes, with real mouse blonde hair, tied into two sweet pigtails that are slightly messy as a real girl's would be, and grey eyes, shiny like wet pebbles. The only way that you know that she is not a real girl is that she is motionless, and a couple of inches smaller in each dimension than a real girl would be.

"Isn't she great?"

"She's *wonderful*."

"I can't believe I managed to get her. It isn't easy to buy this sort of thing."

"I didn't know that you could buy this sort of thing. Didn't know this sort of thing existed."

"I commissioned her. She took months to create. I just got it into my head that I wanted a girl in a glass box."

"But why must she be in a glass box?"

"She is too precious to expose to the air. Fragile. It will keep her safe. If we keep her in there, she might survive a thousand years."

"Stuck in there for all that time. How lonely she'll be."

I feel suddenly terribly sad for the little girl in the dark.

He laughs, triumphantly, because he can hear my sadness and he knows that he's touched me.

But then says quite seriously: "I will look after her you know. She is very precious. And very valuable."

I look at her, standing so calmly in her glass box, and hope that he will.

When Noel defiles my flat, I can't bear to live there even after I have had it professionally cleaned. So the small man offers to let me stay in the corridor room with the little girl. Since I am almost always at work, and very often abroad, I accept.

It is one of the most uncomfortable spaces I have ever lived in. Not because of the little girl, she stands in her case at the dead-end of the room and causes no trouble at all. But the room is impossibly narrow, so narrow that the single futon mattress the small man supplies me with does not fit properly between the two walls and has to be curled up on each side.

This might make for a pleasant cocoon if the mattress was soft, but it isn't soft, it is terribly hard so sleeping in its curl feels like a punishment, like a precursor to being enclosed in concrete. And in the mornings and evenings, as I try to move about the room getting dressed and undressed, I have to walk across the mattress to get anywhere and I stagger on its uneven surface and feel as though I am about to fall.

The contrast between this and the vast, elegant main room that is perpetually being dusted by the Filipino maid, and the little man's perfectly generously sized bedroom and his expensive, inviting bed that the Filipino maid puts fresh sheets on daily, enrages me. As does the contrast between the ill-lit, slightly damp guest bathroom and its ugly soap, and the beautiful bathroom full of exquisite lotions and potions that he has leading off his bedroom.

I am enraged, even though I ought to be feeling

grateful for his hospitality.   But, luckily, I do not see him often so he doesn't seem to notice my ingratitude. He leaves early in the morning to jump about in the park with his personal trainer, and returns late at night after his long run of futile meetings. And even when we are in the flat together, he is constantly on the phone, on the computer, elsewhere, trying to conjure up the magic that will make him feel real.

Then it is his birthday and his excessive busyness is diverted towards the creation of a party. This is activity with which I can sympathise, though I still find myself annoyed by it.

He hires extra staff who in turn seem to be hiring more people: people who can cook, mix cocktails, do dances. He seems both absorbed and irritated by the preparations, and spends much of his time fighting with bureaucrats about whether he can hold the party at the top of the hill in the park opposite the flat. In the end he wins this fight, which seems to satisfy him briefly, but then there are other preparatory battles to fight so he becomes distracted and grouchy again.

As far as I can tell, everyone in the world is being invited.

The party is on a soft cloudy summer night. It is warm but the air feels damp, like rain might come, so I don't try to make myself too exquisite. And, anyhow, I am too tired to make myself exquisite. I am exhausted by flying around the world then returning to the corridor room and the lumpy futon on which I cannot sleep.

It is still light as I climb up the hill to look for the party. I avoid the tarmacked municipal paths that wind gently up the hill and instead take the direct route from the flat to the top of the hill, which happens to be the steepest way. I enjoy feeling my breath labour as I push up the steep slope, the hard thump of my heart. And I like the look of the short grass that I'm walking across, so I stop and take off my silver sandals and then the damp earth dirties my toes as I walk.

It is a strange time of a midsummer night, still light as day, but something imperceptible – perhaps the dying fall of the birdsong – tells me that it is evening, that the light is an impostor, that it is time for evening business. And it gets stranger as I push over the top of the hill, past the little viewing platform where a clump of tourists are gazing down at the ugly city, not much less ugly even at this distance, and see that – just beyond the tourists – a little caravan of party has assembled, a strangely private thing in this public place. Brightly coloured rugs are spread across the grass, gaudy paper lanterns hang in the trees (not yet lit), and pretty young people in comfortable white clothing move gently about between the rugs, offering guests pastel coloured drinks. The little man has created a sort of fairy glade in a municipal park, hanging above the ugly city

I can't see the little man anywhere and I know no-one at the party, so I feel awkward and my feet are cold now from the dampness of the ground and this only adds to my exhaustion so I wonder whether I should leave, just run down the hill and hide in his flat. I am shy like a child at a party and wish that he would come and rescue me from my mawkishness.

But instead of running down the hill, I follow one of the pretty young people in white around until she pauses and then I stutter up to her and ask for a drink and she gives me a pink one and it is, to my tongue, almost unbearably sweet. But I feel better for having something to do, something in my hand, something to numb me a little more.

Eventually I manage to sip the drink down and then I trot after another of the pretty ones in white and I get another drink (turquoise this time) and I see that one of the brightly coloured rugs has no-one sitting on it and it is under a tree with several of the lanterns hanging over it and looks inviting. I go and fold myself down on it, sitting on my feet to keep them warm. And I sip the sweet blue drink and look about me at the other people and try to listen to their conversation.

Everyone seems to be clumped into warm groups of people who know each other well, groups that seem familial even though the people themselves look expensively gaunt and elegant. Some of the groups have dogs in them, and some have pretty children in wonderful outfits, little rock and roll outfits that make them absurdly cool, something about their childishness emphasising the coolness to the point that looking at them almost hurts.

The elegant people in the groups issue little

cries of welcome as they see other people that they also know well, are familiar and warm with, as if everybody here knows everybody else, and - with each little welcoming cry - I feel more alone and more desperate for the small man to come and show me that I am important, even though I do not belong in all this warmth and familiarity.

But he doesn't come, so I sit on the rug alone until the blue drink numbs or warms me, I can't tell which, and the light finally starts to creep away.

As dusk falls, the pretty ones in white start moving among the trees and lighting candles in the paper lanterns. The tourists on the skyline become silhouettes. A handsome group of guests arrives and has nowhere to sit, so they wander up to my rug.

One of them, a dark haired boy, squats down in front of me.

"Would you mind if we sit here too? You do seem to have found a lovely spot."

I feel as though I have forgotten how to speak so I can only nod, and as I do the group settles around me like a flock of birds.

They chatter amongst themselves and I

continue in my silence. Then suddenly: "Why are you so pretty and so alone?" the handsome boy asks.

Even though I am drunk and numb, I think that this is impudent, so I continue in my silence.

"I'm sorry, but everybody here knows everybody, but we don't know you, so we're curious."

"I know the host," I manage.

"Well, we all know him. Everybody knows him. He whirls through all our lives"

"Yes. He does a lot of whirling"

"He does! He does!" The boy laughs, pleased to have got something from me. Then: "My God. You're not her, are you? The one who is living with him?"

I nod and wonder what he means.

He leans back into his flutter of friends.

"Listen, listen everybody, it's her. The one."

He says this as if it is the continuation of a conversation, as if they will know what he means. They stop their fluttering and turn and look and smile brilliantly and some even laugh.

"He's madly in love with you, you know. And we don't think he has ever loved anyone before."

The flutter all smile again, and some of them nod encouragingly.

I look down at my dirty feet in my silver sandals and think how funny it is that he says this as if it is important.

And then a loud ululation soars across the hillside and we hear the other guests cheer and the silhouette of a flailing man flies into the air above the hill.

The African acrobats have started their performance.

After the acrobats, who are wiry brown men with no fat on their bodies, just skin gliding over muscle, the neat little muscles that come from work not working out, fire jugglers light up the dark hill with frightening torches. Then a hula girl swings flashing LED hoops around her powerful hips then up and down her tiny waist. Slashes of light in the darkness.

I am alone again, having wandered off after briefly enjoying the attention from the fluttering friends. I drink another pastel drink (I think it is eau de nil coloured this time, although now it is too dark to be certain) and savour being drunk and the madness of all this display.

"What do you think?"

It is the small man, materializing out of the darkness.

"I think that I don't know why you did this."

"What do you mean?"

"Why would you throw a party like this and then disappear?"

"That's how I like to do it."

"When I throw parties, I want to be at the heart of them. Being adored."

"You are the heart of them, I'm sure."

"But why do you do it?"

"This one was for you. To show you that I can make beauty."

"You left me all by myself. I have been lonely."

"I'm so sorry."

"And there was no-one to adore me."

"But I adore you."

I look down at him and see a man dancing nervously behind his thick black glasses, and I think how luxurious it is, the thought that this has all been done for me, even though I don't think that it is at all beautiful. So I reach out and take one of his surprisingly large strong hands in mine and I pull him along after me and we run straight down the hill together laughing, run away from the guests and the hula dancers and the torches and the lanterns, all the way down into the darkness of the flat (at the back of which lurks the patient little girl). And we pull open the curtains in the big room and see the party still glittering at the top of the hill.

"I am so glad that we are down here in the dark," I say and then finally I let him pull me towards him.

At last, I am sleeping in his big soft bed, draped in the bone dryness of his fine clean linen and I should feel relief, I want to feel relief, but I cannot because – in his sleep – he has thrown himself across the bed diagonally, with his arms flung out, and there is no room, or at least only a corner of room, for me.

I try to rearrange him, to make room for myself, but, each time I do, he spreads himself again, claiming the whole bed. So I try sleeping close to him, my head on his small strong shoulder or my neck on his thick arm but there is no give in him, nowhere comfortable on his body that I can find, no accommodation.

I wake him once, and tell him that he is pushing me out of his bed, and he laughs and says "I'm so sorry beautiful," and sounds as if he means it. A few seconds later, he is asleep again and pushing me away.

This seems to go on for hours. I cannot bear not to sleep in the room, now I am here, so in the end I walk carefully in the dark to the corridor room and get the futon and my old duvet and I drag them into his room and lie the futon along the bottom of his bed. I take one of his pillows with its fine clean linen pillowcase so that I feel a little closer to him and then finally I fall into sleep. My last thought is that I am like a dog, sleeping here at his feet.

In the morning, I expect some change in our relationship, but he just laughs at me and whirls off into his day.

I spend several weeks trying to sleep in his bed and, every night, he pushes me out of the bed and I end up at his feet. His glamorous bedroom is made cluttered and uncomfortable by the lumpy futon, which after a few nights I stop dragging back into the corridor room in the mornings. It is my one grotesque claim on his territory.

During the days, I only pass him briefly in the kitchen, and the Filipino woman is almost always there too, so there is no intimacy. He continues to work late into the evenings and hardly communicates with me while he works, so by the time he comes home I am exhausted by my own work and enraged by his ignoring me and pushing me out of the bed. So we no longer talk or drink or stare out at the hill rising up against the night sky.

I cannot understand why he does not want me now, after all his wanting me. He still claims to want me when I ask him. But I only get a few glancing blows of affection from him so I am starting to wilt.

I corner him in the kitchen one morning. I ignore the Filipino who is polishing a chrome dustbin.

"Why can you never make time for me?"

His eyes stay glued to his phone as he answers. "I shouldn't need to make time for you. We're here together, aren't we?"

"But I want to spend real time with you. Time when I am not being kicked out of bed. We need to have adventures."

"You mustn't be so high maintenance. You know how busy I am."

I am brushed off.

He makes one attempt to mollify me. Takes me to a vastly expensive restaurant on the other side of the city and orders an exquisite fourteen course tasting menu that is cooked and brought to our table by a famous chef. My sleepless exhaustion has brought on a filthy cold and I can smell and taste nothing.

A week later, I leave and go back to the stained nowhere flat, taking the futon with me because I still can't bear to sleep on the mattress that Noel soiled. I am surprised that the small man notices that I'm gone, but he turns up late that night, looking nervous.

"Why have you gone?"

"You gave me no time."

"No. You're right."

"I needed you to make time for me."

"I need someone who doesn't need time."

"I'm not sure if anyone is like that."

"Oh I'm sure I'll find someone."

And with that he leaves, and I feel sad.

The Politician

A war is about to start and everyone is excited. My mother makes placards from old cardboard boxes and takes a coach from her small town to the city to march against the war in a river of hundreds of thousands of other protesters. I march with her but feel detached. I am too exhausted by my own work to properly investigate the case for or against this war, so I do not know enough to protest with any passion.

An old friend of mine is having a party. She is clever and thoughtful and lives and breathes politics. When we were very young, we once had a conversation about how we wanted both to be in politics and to be artists and we decided that we should start with politics as it would be easier to move from that to art than the other way.

She says does not remember the conversation, but she paints pictures that are so beautiful and timeless that when you see them on her wall you think that they must be prints by famous modernist painters.

Usually she keeps her friends in separate groups and I do not meet her political allies, but now she has brought us all together, and the room is full of journalists and policy wonks and even a few real politicians. Rows and rows of champagne flutes are kept filled and we drink from them and talk of nothing but war.

For her party, my friend is wearing a bright red dress. She has pale skin and pale hair and, against this, the red of the dress and the red of her neat lipstick glare vividly. In the past, she worked for a politician who was once a soldier, so she knows more than I do about military matters. She tells me that she thinks the war is a good idea which I find encouraging, since we seem hell-bent on it.

But, as she talks, I am disturbed by the thought of the blood and carnage that lie behind her arguments. She slides off and talks to another guest before I am able to probe her more deeply.

Another friend slips up and hands me a fresh glass of champagne. She points across the room to a tall young man with very neat hair. "That's X," she says. "He was at school with us, but he got a

job with the Prime Minister and now he is an MP".
We laugh wildly because it is absurd that someone
like us should be given so much responsibility. We
still think of ourselves as children, although we are
no longer young.

I look at the man and see him look back at me.
He has a boyish face, with soft edges. A pretty
mouth.

When I am a little drunker, I go and stand near
him. The person he has been talking to walks
away.

"War, then." I say.

"Yes, I think so," he says and he smiles politely
down at me.

"Must we really?"

"We must. The evidence is very strong. He is
terribly dangerous and the diplomacy is getting
nowhere." His voice is tuned to sound quietly
competent, but I can hear the blood thrill echo in
it and again I feel disturbed.

I try to interrogate him for a while but I cannot
shake his confidence, and I do not know enough
about the case against the war to give him any real
discomfort. But, despite the horror circling around
us, I enjoy talking to him. He seems thoughtful

and intelligent, gentle even.

I go back to my girlfriends and we laugh and drink more and try to talk of other things, until the drink runs out and the party is over.

But we are just drunk enough now to want to dance and someone knows of another party where there will be dancing, so we climb into cabs and jig nervously, drunkenly, as we go along and find each other hilarious in our anxiety, which is now no longer about the war but about whether we will find music that we want to dance to and more champagne to drink.

By the time we get to the next party, there is only an hour of it left, and not much alcohol, but we drain what there is and the music is just good enough so we dance forgetfully until it is over.

Then we find ourselves on the cold street and we still need to dance and drink more, and I realise that we are quite near the nowhere flat so I call to the others and ten or more of us roll down the city and up my stairs. I have a bottle of vodka that we swig and pass around.

The MP is with us and seems as wild and drunk as the rest of us now. We play trashy pop music and stalk around the stark flat laughing when we fall over. He and I stalk together and shout the lyrics of a ridiculous rock song about love. I am delighted at how abandoned he is. We all are. It is as if we've danced the war away.

Then everybody leaves and I understand that he is going to stay and I am pleased because he is tall and thoughtful and abandoned.

We sit on the floor together, leaning against the battered green sofa, just opposite the white rabbit, who hasn't minded all the dancing because she is safely in her cage. She sits neatly on her hay and fixes her pink eyes on us.

I offer him the dregs of the vodka bottle.

"No thank you. I don't drink after midnight any more. That way I can cope with the next day's work. Otherwise I really couldn't."

So I drink the dregs instead.

We talk. He tells me that he has just left a girlfriend who didn't excite him enough. He says that he wants to come home from work in the evening and be inspired. This seems to me like a rather calculating way to think about a lover or a wife. As if this woman would have a function: to be inspiring. But it is late and I am drunk so I don't think too deeply about this.

There is a lull in the conversation, so I think about kissing him, but then his phone rings. He apologizes and says that it is an old friend, one of the women who had been dancing in the flat with us and that he must answer it in case she is in trouble, so late at night.

It turns out that she has lost her wallet, and thinks that she must have left it in the flat. So she comes back in and talks to us for a while. She is tall like him, tall and beautiful with enormous eyes. I do not know her well. Many of my friends do but I have always been frightened by her. When I was young, I had a boyfriend who went to her school and was obsessed by her and ambivalent about me. Back then she was a poet and a DJ in New York which was impossibly glamorous, so I understood his obsession but it still fucked me up.

Tonight, though, she is tired and gentle and paces around the kitchen drinking water and talking about how fun the evening has been. She says that it has been the most fun she has had for a while, but there is a catch in her voice and I can tell that she hasn't forgotten the war.

Eventually she leaves and I am pleased as it means that I can finally kiss him.

We go to bed and talk and fuck all night. We tell each other a great deal. It is a serious conversation, but gentle. It feels as though we are exploring one another. Or perhaps interviewing.

He hopes that his party does not stay in power for too long, says that he would like to be in opposition so that he could have a quieter life, get married and have children. I like his detachment. I tell him that I find it hard to take my work seriously, that I have to be ridiculous and wild at night in proportion to the seriousness of my work in the day. He laughs and I think he understands.

In the early hours of the morning, we sleep briefly, and then he has to get up and go to work. We decide to go for a coffee to help shake us into life. I suddenly feel terrible and he offers to carry me to the café. I think this is a wonderful offer but I manage to walk on my own feet.

Two weeks later he emails me to say that he has fallen in love with someone else. Strangely, he asks to meet to discuss this.

We have lunch in the anonymity of a museum restaurant, under a mural of mutant fairy tales painted by a woman whose husband took years to die slowly in her arms. The fairy tales are disturbing, not pretty.

The MP is awkward. Or rather he is stilted, unpleasantly distant, as if he wishes that he wasn't here. I can't imagine why he is. Before coming, I had faintly romantic notions, that he might tell me that I was wonderful, nearly right, almost the one. When I am sitting across a small glass table from him, I see that this is exactly what he plans to tell me, but that this is not romantic at all but simply grotesque.

The woman he has fallen in love with is the woman who left her wallet in my flat, the beautiful woman with the huge eyes who paced uneasily before the war.

I try to smile and congratulate him, but I want to leave and I cannot swallow my food.

I am sure she will be interesting.

A month later, I visit some friends who live in a pretty flat with a fireplace, high up in an old house. Several people are gathered there, sitting on the floor around the fireplace. Many of them know the MP and they are laughing about him as I come in.

"Ah, there you are," the owner of the fireplace says as I walk in. "We are laughing about the MP. He came to supper last night and proudly told us that he fell in love with the filmmaker that night before the war that we all danced at your flat."

"Ah," I say.

"We laughed at him because we all know that he fell in love with you that night."

I am stupidly grateful for this.

Transvestite

The boy stalks into the nightclub with his entourage behind him. His face is hidden beneath the hood of an elaborately embroidered robe. He climbs onto the stage and starts to sing whining, grinding pop music. He is tall and blonde and thin and his shoulders are so broad that they are almost like wings. Everyone in the room watches him. His beauty stabs at them from under the hood.

The keyboard player is a voluptuous red-head. She wears a basque on which the boy's name is spray-painted, black letters sprawling across her breasts. She grinds her hips and tosses her hair, her face blank.

After two songs, the boy throws back his hood and glares archly at the crowd. He purses his lips and launches into another song during which he throws off the robe and we see that his taut, skinny body is slung about with the straps of a jewelled wrestling suit.

Watching him, something wild thrums through my veins.

After the set, I go to the bar. Another beautiful boy with dark hair and pencilled eyes, and an undead look about him, stands next to me as I order my drink. We kiss without speaking to one another, a passionate licking kiss, then peel off back into the crowd. I find the performing boy and dance with him. A wild dance of display. We draw a crowd around us. We are magnetic, electric.

The next day, I get home from work to find a CD waiting on my doormat. On the cover, the boy sits naked and golden, looking up at the camera from under his fringe. He has written a message to me in black marker across his chest.

"I want to know you."

I let the boy suck me into a nightlife that I had not known existed. People dressed as fierce, mythical creatures. Horns attached to their heads, faces hidden behind elaborate masks of makeup, boys in skirts.

Sometimes the boy is a beautiful boy,

sometimes he is a spectacular woman. I find him breathtaking; I want to become him, to ride through the night on his impossibly broad, delicate shoulders.

One night, he wears six inch go-go dancers shoes with transparent platforms and a huge Russian fur hat. His face is painted to look exactly like a beautiful woman, nothing like the caricature of drag, and with the shoes and the hat he floats above the crowd, ethereal and elongated.

I trail in his wake, a small dark thing, feeling powerful because we are together, because his hand wraps around mine and pulls me behind him.

Arab

I am drunk at an opulent restaurant in the middle of the city. I am dragged to a party in a small flat, also opulent. In the small flat there is an enormous man smiling wildly at me. His smile is enormous too, teeth so white, like lightening. I don't know why he is smiling at me.

I say goodbye. He comes to the door with me, huge, overwhelming. Gazing down at me. Says that I am *so beautiful*. I am mystified.

The giant wants to take me away. Issues an invitation of great courtesy. We will go to his family home in the Middle East. We go. Travelling with him is like riding on the back of an elephant.

There are acres of white marble and heaped bowls of pistachios, macadamias, almonds. A lift to the roof, where I sunbathe alone. A younger cousin (who must do what the giant tells him because he is the younger cousin) drives me to ruins, buys me kebabs when I am hungry.

At night, the giant returns to tell me stories and feed me sweetmeats and milky Arak. I lie on his bed and he massages my back. A canopy of white muslin encloses us.

One day, I am swept through the strange streets in his wake to a pet shop where we play with monkeys and parrots.

Another day, we drive to the Dead Sea and float our beautiful bodies. My head slips underwater. The salt daggers into my eyes and nose.

In the dark of a hotel, he kisses me. I am mystified. I know he has had thousands of lovers. He has made himself enormous, filled himself with testosterone to attract countless men.

We drive to the top of a hill, a biblical site. The giant points across the Dead Sea to his real home. Gaza. His enormous eyes fill with enormous tears.

We sweep down the dry country past nomads and checkpoints and machine-guns. The giant tells me about the beauty of the Wadis in spring. Flowers and bird song in the green trees. In his dreams. Here everything is dry.

We go to the pink city and I nearly burst with

delight as we gallop perfect horses through the sand, try to charm camels and climb and climb through the desert–traders' intricate ruins.

Then he takes me to the airport, waves goodbye and disappears for two years.

After which the giant tears back into my life, ripping through the wall of forgetfulness that I have built while he was away, full of apology, brimming with love.

This time, I eye him like prize cattle. We eye each other like breeding stock.

We wind about each other in bed, trying to catch hold. To find a hold that will keep us entwined.

He takes me to Egypt. In the backstreets, he has my name inscribed in Arabic script on the leather binding of an empty book. We ride horses through the pyramids, pay our respects to the Sphinx. Imagine our wedding ceremony in an empty hotel at the edge of the desert, choose which of the elegant French houses of Old Cairo we want to live in. I am greedy for this future, tucked away in an Arab household with monkeys to keep me company. Back in my city we have dinner with some of my gay friends. Afterwards, after he disappears, one tells me that he had already met the giant. Had been on a date with him. I assume this means that he has fucked him.

We go to Paris. He takes me to Dior, Hermes, Fauchon. At each shop he buys me something, at each shop I want more than he buys me. But it is exhilarating. In our exquisite hotel room we laugh with delight at my array of crisp, branded bags. But I wish the hotel was even more exquisite. This is a transaction and I do not believe that he is giving me sufficient camels in return for my life.

After Paris, he disappears again. At first he calls me regularly, full of apologies, he is stuck at home, the family business needs him. Then he tells me that he is going to the Libyan desert to do an oil deal, that calling me will be difficult for a while.

And then there is silence. I believe he has smelt my greed and been sickened by it. I cannot blame him.

Woodsman

The Singer introduced us. I cannot think about either of them without crying.

Shadows under blue eyes, when we first meet he disappears his beauty into the pub gloom so that I hardly notice it. Says he's exhausted from working nights on the underground lines. Keeps a step back from the conversation. I am still obsessed by the Singer so I pay no attention to amazing eyes, a fine bald head, slabs of muscle. Later, I watch *Apocalypse Now* and am moved to tears to see him, it must be him, they are so alike when the actor is bald, rotting and sweating in the heart of that fictional darkness.

When we meet, I feel immediately that he is an ally. He has seen the Singer's madness play out before and pities me.

And it does play out and I am torn apart and so I call the Woodsman again and again. He listens patiently as I yowl with pain. He is gentle, soothing, tolerant as if he is dealing with a wild thing who has stuck its foot in a trap. Yowling at him, who knows, who has seen it all before and so understands, soothes me. So I do it again and again.

He lives in a single room with some books on trees, a small television, and a set of weights. At dawn, he cycles ten miles to the top of a hill at the edge of the city where he spends the day shaping trees. He cycles back again before dusk and lifts weights until he is too tired to move. At the weekend, he sometimes drinks with the Singer, but otherwise he does not go out. He lives frugally and spends what little spare money he has on drugs. He has no girlfriends.

He visits me at the centre of the city. We drink beer at my favourite pub. Eat burgers at the same diner that I used to go to with Noel. Being with him soothes me. We talk endlessly about the Singer and say little about ourselves. All I really know about him is that he once had long hair and did nothing at all, not even the little he does now, until his aggressive, overbearing father, who was a policeman, abandoned his mother and left the Woodsman feeling liberated. And then, even though he had gone, he felt that he needed to show his father that he could do something – so he started to take care of trees, even though the father was no longer there to see it.

He loves the trees. This is wonderful. This and his blue eyes and his Brando nose. Soothing. And he is funny. Absurd. He veers from quick wit to doltishness, happy to play my fool.

I am being soothed, and he leaves his room a little more frequently to neither work or take drugs. Our meetings become very regular: we dilute one another's loneliness. I decide that I am in love with him. I tell the Singer, who laughs. I can see no reason why the Woodsman and I should not be perfectly happy. I know that he loves me and he has told me that he thinks I am beautiful.

We go to a house-party at the edge of the city. A wild party in a sad house. The married couple who live in it have tried to have babies for ten years. But there are no babies here.

I am brown from the Italian sun. I wear white trousers and a white vest. Everyone at the party is shocked to see me in anything other than black. I smile and drink and tell stories about my adventures with the Singer.

The Woodsman is there, quiet, at the edge of things. I feel that he is not only shrinking away from the party, but from me. I cannot see why. I pin him down briefly:

"Come outside with me."

"Why would I want to do that?"

I cannot answer, not here. Awkwardness between us for the first time.

Late now and I have collapsed on the marriage bed, the bed without babies. My left sinus is swollen and blood bangs painfully behind my left eye, something that happens when I drink poisonous amounts of alcohol. I rub my face with my drunken palm, cocooned here in the bedroom away from them all. I feel like a white slug on the couple's floral bed linen.

I am still focused on my target though. My new love. And, wonderfully, he comes into the bed-room. I haul myself up from the crumpled floral sheets and demand that he stays, but he goes. So I crawl off the bed and creep after him, corner him in the bathroom and announce my love. He goes.

When the poison has flushed out of me, I call him.

"Why not?" I ask. "Why on earth should we not?"

"It just doesn't feel right." He cannot answer clearly.

"I love you. Don't you love me? I am sure you love me."

"I do."

"Then why not?"

"It would be madness."

"Why?"

"We are too different."

"How?"

"You must be mad if you can't see it."

After this, six months of silence. We are careful never to be alone together.

Something shifts.

We meet again at the pub at Christmas time. It is the Christmas that I will spend with Noel. I have given up on Christmas but here is my gift. Embodied in flesh and blood as a true Christmas present ought to be.

Everything is as it was before but, because he is

here again after the silence, it is all different. This time the evening will end up with us together on the green leather sofa in the nowhere flat. This time I will be wrapped in his arms all night, talking about the future that we are going to make.

It has all been set up for us, prepared. An imaginary nest is ready for us to move into. Built from my longing and his emptiness.

I spend New Year in the cheap sun of the Canary Islands. The second half of my escape from celebration, this time with a girlfriend who also has cause to escape. We are on a mystery holiday as it is even cheaper that way, and do not know where the holiday company will send us until the bus stops at a small hotel by the sea at the edge of a concrete sprawl. I know that the interior of this island is beautiful, honey farms and thyme scented. We will not taste or smell this, but we are grateful that we are at the edge of the sprawl, not in its centre.

In the centre is a hell of cheap English Breakfasts and synthetic cocktails. We wander through it as the New Year begins, wondering why we are here and how we can escape. The Woodsman calls and I am saved. Then guilty because my girlfriend does not have her own lifeline.

Back in the freezing city, I watch him for a minute in an underground station before he sees me. Wrapped in a leather jacket, hat, gloves, scarf he seems less heroic than in my imagination. For a moment, I wonder whether I can really love him. Then he sees me. Comes up and stands close in front of me, looks down over the bundle of his scarf and laughs.

We spend three days in bed, fending off the cold, drinking tea and laughing. On the second day, I break down. It is impossible that I have found a harbour at last. I am still adrift in a small boat on a frozen sea, dreaming. He stands seriously in his small bedroom, a statue again, and tells me that he will never ever leave me. Apparently I am not dreaming. I am parked, docked, home.

It is a leap year. Just before midnight on Valentine's Day, I ask the Woodsman to marry me. He says yes and we curl together in delight. But we do not tell anyone of our engagement.

I am desperate to make our home a concrete thing. Because I know he will not move far from his familiar places, and because we are very poor (I am no longer taking my work seriously), we decide to live in an ugly suburb at the edge of the city. It is far away from my friends, from where I was born, where I have lived. But it is near the Singer and his pub. Near that bonhomie, so I believe that we can be happy.

I find us a large, cheap mansion flat high above the southern edge of the city(south, not where I belong). Four stories up at the top of a hill. A main road runs beneath us, constantly grinding with traffic. This road is lined with terrible shops and fast food joints, places for the poor to subsist from. The building, the hallways and the flat itself are all painted a dirty, pissy yellow-white. The curtains and carpets are yellow-brown.

But it is huge, and we can see for miles from the windows. We move in, the Woodsman and I and my white rabbit. Almost immediately the rabbit starts ripping the lining paper off the wall, at the point where it meets the skirting board. She works her way rapidly around the bottom edge of every wall in the flat, so that soon each room has a jagged edge. The vast expanses give her a wider range than she is used to, and she soon becomes almost feral, spending days on end hiding in the cardboard box houses that we make to help her feel less daunted by all this space.

Now I feel even more nowhere than I was before, but we laugh constantly. He is brilliantly funny: absurd, playful, grotesque. When we are alone, his comic genius takes over our life. I am the only member of his audience, and every performance is carefully honed to delight and divert me. When we are not laughing, we talk in our own private language which is all absurd affection. I am proud that this is ours alone.

We are almost always alone. The only person from the centre of the city who follows me here is the transvestite boy. I thought he was only interested in me because of the glamour of my flat, and the people I knew when I was in the centre who might have helped him to become famous. Now I am here I have nothing of that sort to offer him, so I assume that he will disappear. But still he calls, visits, is kind. I am surprised.

We are too poor to go out. Too poor to go to the pub even. Our treats are cheap vodka and

Kentucky Fried Chicken on Saturday nights. I also like wandering the aisles of the local supermarket. Buying anything, even the food that we need to stay alive, is a thrill.

We stop fucking almost as soon as we move in together. He stops fucking me. On weekdays it is impossible. He gets up at 5am to cycle to the trees and collapses into bed after supper. But every weekend I try to seduce him. He will not respond.

I stop trying after two months. Being in bed together becomes something to endure. The beautiful body that I am not allowed to touch and the traffic crashing past below the flat stop me sleeping until the early hours, then thin curtains let the light in and wake me at dawn. Eventually, I find that, if I wrap my eyes in a mask and stuff my ears with plugs, I can get some sleep. Cocooned in darkness and silence, separate from him.

But I do not think of leaving.

I work from home with only the rabbit for company. She behaves as if she is terrified of me most of the time, but occasionally we find ourselves in one of the smaller rooms together (she favours the toilet and my study) and she flops herself over onto her side, inviting me to stroke her feather-soft belly. Having eaten all of the wallpaper that she can reach, she starts eating electric wires. She manages to destroy the internet and phone lines. I think she wants me to be as isolated as she is.

I am very isolated. It takes three bus rides to get into the centre of the city, with a long cold wait between each ride. I go down there less and less. After a day alone in the piss grey skylight of the flat I am thrilled when the Woodsman comes home. He is always charming, even though he is exhausted. As soon as he walks through the door he becomes one of his comic characters, usually a childish dolt. The dolt and I play peek-a-boo around one or other of the many door-frames. This and the first vodka are the highlights of my day.

We keep laughing in our piss-yellow eerie until a letter arrives telling us that our landlord has decided to sell the flat and wants us to move out. I am excited. I want us to move to the north of the city where I was born, where there are green hills and good transport links. But the Woodsman categorically refuses to go there, even for an afternoon. He has never been there and never wants to.

I adjust my ambitions. Start hunting for something nearer to the city, but still close to his patch. This seems like such an obvious solution that I cannot believe it when he resists. I cajole him for a few weeks, try laughing him out of it, but he remains in sullen opposition. Then I become furious and demand that he makes allowances for what I need. What I want. Some closer contact with the outside world if not with him.

I win the battle. But the laughter stops for a month. And the laughter is pretty much all that we have.

We move into the basement of an eighteenth century townhouse a little closer to the centre of the city, its grand symmetry painted white and set back from the road. The townhouse is on the edge of what has until recently been an immigrant slum, and is one of several old landmarks that stick up amongst the street markets and bars like old fossils in a swamp.

The area turns my stomach, but I am glad of the beauty of the house and the underground station, five minutes' walk away, feels like a lifeline.

Our basement is dingy and damp when we visit it, but the rooms feel human and intimate after the too-large spaces in the sky. And outside the kitchen and bedroom windows there is a small garden. The estate agent promises that the flat will be painted any colour we choose. I choose white, wanting to wash away the pissy yellow that has gone sour. As we prepare for the move, I dream of this new underground nest, glowing white and clear. The Woodsman glowers and sulks but I hold tight to the thought of a quiet, brilliantly white home, bulbs pushing through the soil in its garden.

On the day that we move we arrive at the house, to find that they have painted it piss-cream, not white. I hide behind a pile of boxes in the bedroom and cry.

But it is a fresh start. It must be. I forgive him.

I want a ring. An old, battered ring in soft gold with a pearl in it. On the internet, I find rings like this, old rings that seem to tell beautiful stories but cost almost nothing. I show him. Even he could afford them. It is Christmas again and I tell him this is all that I want. To have his ring on my finger. I want the glamour of marriage to gild our poverty.

I give him a telescope. He does not give me a ring.

But we are in the countryside, in my mother's old house, with her old dog and a Christmas tree covered in birds and I, like the birds, feel light and perched somewhere beautiful. During advent I decorate a tree in our basement with the ornaments that I have been collecting all my life. I have made the basement beautiful and the Christmas things make it even more so. Things glow. The laughter comes back.

Every night in our quiet, dark, underground bedroom, I cradle his beautiful bald head like a baby. I stroke him to sleep in my arms and feel euphoric, some hormonal response to the cradling singing in my veins in the pitch blackness. I have learnt how to hold him like this, so closely, without troubling him. From the ribcage down, our bodies never touch, our sexual organs always angled gently away to avoid contact.

I always hold him. I am always soothing him. I am no longer soothed by him.

But not every night. On Saturday nights, the Singer comes to our house to drink cheap beer with him, to drink beer and smoke weed and snort whatever they can afford.

I hide in the bedroom and long for him to come to me.

Instead, after the Singer has left, he stays up all night playing computer games, wired. He is a crack warrior fighting horrifying creatures in an alien landscape.

I try to sleep, aching for him, as gunfire and explosions echo round the flat.

Then the laughter comes back with even more intensity. I am even more intensely delighted to see him when he comes home to me, comes down the outside steps into our subterranean place. His clowning has evolved and refined into something that can almost immediately make me dissolve hopelessly into laughter. I am never allowed to stop laughing.

The laughter starts to disturb me.

It is Valentine's Day again. This is the longest I have ever spent with a man. The beginning of forever, I still think, though with a growing feeling of unease. I decide to buy the Woodsman and the rabbit a special present.

The rabbit is less feral in the new place, we keep her in one room, my study, so that we can protect the walls. We have lined the room with hardboard to just over the height of a rabbit standing on its back legs. But she seems listless and bored in this smaller space. I want her to be happy.

I go to the pet shop in a famous department store. They have a glass-fronted cage full of tiny white rabbits. Lop-eared, pink-eyed slugs. I watch them carefully for a while, then choose the only rabbit that stays fast asleep the whole time that I watch. A calm companion for my nervy female. I buy the little slug and take him home in a cardboard box with holes cut in it so that he can breathe. He doesn't seem to mind the taxi ride at all so I take him out of the box and sit him on my lap as we travel through the city.

When the Woodsman comes home that night, I sit him down on the sofa and make him close his eyes with his hands spread open on his lap. I take the rabbit out of its box, and sit him in the Woodsman's hands. The Woodsman opens his eyes, they widen with delight. The rabbit is still small enough to fit easily in the palm of one of his hands. We put him on the floor and he noses around, rubbing his chin on everything he encounters. Then, suddenly, he does a twisting, kicking leap of joy and scarpers across the room.

Both rabbits must be de-sexed if they are to live together without producing babies and anyhow the vet tells me that if I don't spay the female rabbit she will have an eighty percent chance of getting womb cancer. He tells me that rabbits are so engineered for fertility that if they are not given babies, they grow their own little death-baby tumours.

The female is terribly weakened by the operation and I am afraid that she is going to die. She refuses to eat for several weeks. Eventually we let her play with the boy rabbit, who is growing rapidly. They do a wild and impossibly fast circling dance at the end of which he leaps onto her back. He is absurdly quick for a little slug. After this she starts eating again. Flesh covers her delicate bones.

She often grooms him, holding his long ears up between her paws so that she can lick the insides clean. He never grooms or licks her except by mistake, if he confuses her soft white fur with his own.

I am laughing more than I ever have before, but I feel dead. At night, after I have stroked the Woodsman asleep in my arms and he has rolled over to sleep with his back turned to me, as he always does, I get up and wander through the dark basement and feel like a ghost wandering through my own life. It feels alien, like some dangerous parallel reality.

I know that the things that surround me are mine. These pictures on the walls are mine. This kitchen is mine, where I cook daily, this rug rough under my bare feet. But I feel disconnected from it all, there is a chasm between myself and all this that makes me dizzy. Through the chasm slips the fear of death. Some absence here terrifies me and reminds me that there will be another larger, longer emptiness.

But as I walk at night through darkness and the stripes of moonlight that find their way through the shutters, I feel strangely liberated. Nothing

holds me down. No-one tries to make me laugh. I
am free to feel the bleakness.

I often sleep on the sofa, comforted by the way
the soft upholstery wraps around me, pushing my
arms into my body until I am wrapped up in
myself.

Then I have lunch with No-name who makes me
realize that I do not need to feel dead and I decide
to leave. I tell the Woodsman. He is furious at
first, glowing with cold anger.

"Why?"

"Because I feel dead."

"Why do you feel dead?"

"Because you never fuck me. Because I cannot
live in a world as small as this one."

"Is it so small?"

"You are not small, but your orbit is. I need to
range further."

"Where do you want to go?"

"I want to go north of the city. You would never
even visit the north with me. "

"I will go north with you now."

"I don't believe you."

He comes north with me once, after we have already agreed that it is over. It is an unseasonably warm spring day, and we lie in the grass together, looking down over the city. Everything is perfect for that day. We know everything so nothing can hurt us. He is amazed by the beauty of the green spaces of the north, full of regret that he did not come here with me sooner. I lie quietly in his arms, the sun beating down on us in our peaceful grief.

As soon as it is over, as soon as he knows that really it is over, he is able to fuck me again. We cry as we fuck, looking into one another's eyes.

He tells me that he could not fuck me before because I was too precious. I had transformed his life in a way that he had thought impossible, and in doing so I became something more than his lover and he could not touch me.

I know that I could stay. But I can still feel the tall walls that enclose his world stretching up around us and so I escape.

No-name

The wind blew constantly and my halls of residence were right beside an abattoir. I had spent all my money and had to steal food from the supermarkets. One night I had the worst dream of my life. In it, a tramp killed my father by stabbing his eyes with a broken bottle. I woke up and escaped my bedroom, walked the dark corridors of the residence until dawn, listening to the wind, still terrified.

The next day I saw No-name for the first time. He was eating in the university cafeteria and I engineered a meeting. He had a long, fresh scar running down his beautiful dark face. He told me that the night before he had been wandering the streets of Paris with his friends, drunk and happy, and had run into a tramp who was sleeping in a square with a fountain in the middle of it. The tramp smashed the bottle that No-name had been drinking from and slashed him across the face with it.

I told him about my dream then traced the tape covering the scar with my finger as we sat in the evening sunlight outside the cafeteria. The wind dropped for a moment, then resumed, blowing dust from the concrete floor into our eyes.

He was studying mime. His work involved total control of his body, easy control of every bone and muscle. He could flip and twist, becoming first this metaphor (a toppling building) then that (an opening rose). But when he stopped moving and started thinking, he would freeze. It was as if he had climbed into some invisible coffin and the lid had slammed down on him.

When I first saw him lie immobilised like this, on a single bed in an anonymous university bedroom, I asked him what he was thinking. He told me that death terrified him. His death. Not anybody else's.

I felt a profound sense of relief.

Then he pushed up out of his coffin and started moving again, shaking death off.

He took me to a party full of other actors,

*singers, dancers. One woman was completely
naked but painted as if an ivy-vine trailed around
her body. Talking Heads was playing.*

*When I looked into his eyes, they looked like
my eyes.*

I ran away.

Many years later, we meet again. No-name is
married to a dancer and I think he is happy. This
pleases me.

But, one night, No-name takes me out to dinner
and then kisses me impetuously while we stand at
the crowded bar of my favourite pub. Afterwards,
as we walk through the tunnels of an underground
station, he starts to cry with regret at not having
married me.

Two nights later, he takes me out to dinner
again. His neck is covered with dark purple
bruises given to him by a whore that he has visited
since I last saw him. This does not stop me
believing him when he says that he loves me.

No-name and I are two halves of the same
thing. No-name thinks I am brilliant and I become
brilliant when I am with him. I know he is broken.

Fear still lurks beneath his vivid exterior. I love the fear.

He is as frightened by death as I am. More so. My panic has subsided, but his still overwhelms and incapacitates. He finds my familiarity with the panic soothing. He is not alone in it. And neither, briefly, am I, as night after night we cleave together hopelessly in dark rooms, knowing that we have no future.

But No-name is an explosion. His pyrotechnic display lights up my life. After No-name kisses me, I feel like I can flatten mountains and give birth to a universe. And so No-name and I don't come to nothing after all.

Home

I am still touched by the tendrils of affection that
the transvestite boy sent into my exile with the
Woodsman. When I leave, when No-name lib-
erates me, I decide that I want to live with the
transvestite and his boy, a gentle quiet creature
who follows him around nightclubs dressed as a
sailor. I think that together we might build
something beautiful. Something beautiful and
loose and open, nothing like the tight insularity
that I am escaping.

I invite the transvestite to tea. A glamorous tea
that marks the end of my exile. He wears a
beautiful white suit and looks delicate and a bit
fragile against the black lacquer panels of the tea-
room. He has shadows under his eyes. But as I ask
him whether he will live with me, his face lights
up. He seems as thrilled as I am at the thought. He
has been living in the basement of a Finnish
alcoholic, and he cannot wait to escape her

disasters and clinging.

In springtime, we hunt for our home. Magnolias blossom on bare branches.

We want to live north of the city, near the green hills. The transvestite was born on a farm amongst fields of herbs and now he is sickened by the city's dirt. He wants to live in a village.

At the end of our second day of hunting, we find it. An enormous basement flat at the bottom of a vast old mansion at the top of a hill. It has huge white spaces, tiled and blank, and a small patio, and the elderly Chinese landlord says we can have pets. We manage to scrape together a pile of cash and pay the deposit immediately.

Our new home is a short walk from the mansion block that I lived in as a young child. It is in a part of the city that really was once a quiet village, and has winding walkways and ancient houses that seem to sit in a pile on top of one another as they climb the sides of the hills. The walkways eventually lead to a heath which feels almost wild and has distant views of the city's sprawl. Everywhere we go is partly familiar. My memory is stirred.

Although nothing is the size that I remember it.

High walls and long walkways that used to engulf me are now shorter, narrower and less magical. But I am still able to get lost on the heath. It hasn't lost its weirdness. I still feel as though strange creatures might live in its copses and woodlands and lakes.

I am pleased by the blankness of our new home. White tiles, white walls, everything lit by fluorescent strips. There is almost no natural light.

My room is right at the back of the flat and is reached by its own private corridor, a sort of tunnel that must bridge some bit of the old house's foundations. The tunnel is raised up by a few feet and has a long clothes rail running along the right hand side and a tiny bathroom to the left. At the end of this tunnel, at night, my room is completely dark and quiet except for the occasional deep rumbling from a train tunnel that burrows under the building. I find the darkness terrifying and there is no one to cling onto, no human flesh to reassure me. But when the lights are on, I enjoy being buried and separated off.

The transvestite and his boy have a bedroom

that is much closer to the light. It opens onto the main living space, near the vast sliding glass walls that are our front door. So they are like sentries, guarding the entrance. And I am a girl in a trance. They are so grateful for having been brought up the hill and out of the city to this wonderful place that I feel that they do really want to make themselves into my guardians. Other than when I turn out the light in my windowless bedroom, I feel surrounded by warm protection.

Since the whole place is crepuscular, the rabbits are happy. Dusk and dawn are their favourite times of day: here it is always dusk, always dawn. And they have much more room to roam. The walls are painted plaster so there is no wallpaper for them to rip down. The smoothness of the floor-tiles makes it hard for them to accelerate, but they find enough friction on the doormat for the occasional leap. They spend most of their time behind a pile of suitcases, ripping apart old cardboard boxes that we have put there for them.

Once or twice a day they hop around the flat, marking their territory with their chins and chewing books and furniture. They look beautiful in all the whiteness: soft white against hard white.

Suddenly I am given a large amount of money. A man gives it to me, an acquaintance who is clinically insane. Abundance after famine. It does not occur to me that I should save or invest it since I do not feel that I have a future to invest for and I immediately spend it all.

I buy a very long black sofa covered in soft black calves' leather, long enough for two couples to stretch out on and fuck at the same time, toe to toe. A dining room table made of dense oak sleepers that sucks away cares and fear when you lean on it. A battered suede easy chair that enfolds you so comfortably that sitting in it I fall asleep within minutes. A huge sheepskin rug – made from the skins of eight sheep – soft and big enough for us all to lie on together and dissolve into. And the most beautiful wooden French bed, gilt-painted, with a lacy wicker headboard topped by tumbling carved garlands of flowers and leaves. A grandiose bed for enchanting men.

I also buy wonderful clothes. Strange and sculptural dresses, jackets tailored on Eighteenth century patterns, nipping in my waist and emphasising my breasts. Leggings that send strange organic ruffles curling around my calves and thighs. Boots in soft leather, with hooks and eyes up the back like a Victorian urchin's. All in black as my clothes have always been. But still, a new wardrobe for my new life. For hunting new men.

We throw a house-warming party. Each of us is equally pleased with our new home and we want to show it off. We string neon lights around the vast living space, roll up the sheepskin rug and lock the rabbits up for the night. Buy cases of champagne and rent boxes of champagne glasses. We never return the glasses. We know that there will be more parties.

I invite everyone I know and so does the transvestite. His boy has very few friends. The transvestite's guests are a mixture of performance artists, aged supermodels, Buddhist actresses and old queens who worship his boyish beauty. His guest of honour is a famous homosexual who was imprisoned in the Fifties for seducing a boy. He is very old and sits in the corner being paid homage to by the young queers.

All my old friends have come to the party and No-name is my guest of honour. My friends seem as ecstatic as I am to find me living here in this

strange bunker. Brought back from the dead by
the beautiful queer boys.

We start the evening by playing Ziggy
Stardust. The transvestite is both Ziggy and Lady
Stardust. I am a Suffragette from the City. He is
dressed in a wildly decorated track-suit and wears
light make-up: he is a boy this evening though the
ghost of his feminine self hovers. I wear one of his
jackets: it has 'Fuck the World' graffitied on the
back.

We whirl and twirl amongst our guests. There
are many strangers: since we want new blood, we
told our guests to bring people that we don't know.
Outside in our tiny garden, a dark-haired opera
singer with paper-white skin talks to a fake-tanned
rent-boy while the MP and his magnificent fiancée
stalk across the dance floor that we have created
where the sheepskin rug normally lies. We play
mad bad cheap pop-music and it combines with
the champagne to create a perfect storm of crazy
dancing. I head-bang and leap to Van-Halen with
a boy with long hair that whips about him as we
dance, then the transvestite whirls me in his arms
to Britney Spears' *Toxic*.

Two of my girlfriends do a choreographed stalk

across the dance floor to *A Town Called Malice*, then split up and are swept away by men who want to kiss them. I continue to stomp about triumphantly. This is my home, my party, my ecstatic whirl.

Through the champagne fog, I feel No-name watching me. Feel him encouraging my wildness. He approves of what I am creating. I know that he will shortly be leaving me. I think that he is pleased at the thought that, when he goes, I will still be surrounded by this beautiful chaos. I go and stand with him between fits of dancing, warming myself on our connection, catching my breath.

Eventually the party starts to die down. The champagne is running out and people are exhausted from all the dancing but there are couples kissing on the long sofa. The transvestite and I have had enough now and we kick them out. His boy is dead drunk, already passed out on their bed. But the transvestite is fairy-like, light on his feet and alert. We grin at each other, agreeing that it is all wonderful. He wraps me in his arms, kisses the top of my head and goes off to undress the boy.

One of my girlfriends emerges from the dark

garden with a friend of No-name's. I love them both and think they are a good match, so I ask them to stay. We find a bottle of champagne that I have hidden and retreat into my bedroom. No-name is waiting on the golden bed. The four of us sit in a drunken circle on the bed-throne in the deep subterranean darkness. Gradually conversation mutates into kissing. I pull a spare mattress out for the other couple, then melt into No-name.

It is pitch dark and I can see nothing, but I can feel him looking at me intensely. "I adore you," he says, through the dark. It feels like he is branding me.

When No-name leaves me, I am not destroyed, because I knew that he would leave me. Part of the joy that was between us was predicated on the fact that he would. I write him a poem. The words contain my grief.

When he is gone, my life with the boys can blossom. We nest together: our days become as domesticated as our nights are wild. The transvestite is terrified of getting old or fat and so spends a great deal of time and effort on making violently healthy meals. Fruit smoothies for breakfast, heaps of complicated salads at lunchtime, fresh and lean evening meals. We all feed each other, and frequently cook ourselves formal suppers, with several courses, which we eat sitting around the heavy oak table, just like a family. The boys eat vast amounts very quickly. I eat much less, slowly, enjoying their easy companionship. I like feeling nourished and accepted.

The transvestite is also preoccupied with his spiritual health. He sporadically adheres to many different beliefs and is sometimes Buddhist. During the Buddhist phases, he chants in his bedroom every morning. The purpose of this chanting is not some abstract transcendence – he does it because he believes it will get him what he wants.

The bedroom walls are very thin, so the sound of his voice, made deep and resonant for the sake of the chanting, resonates around the flat, punctuated by the ringing of his little brass bell. His voice sometimes sounds whiny and disapproving, as if he were admonishing the

Buddha or some wider life-force for not doing his bidding. When he is not being Buddhist he talks about star-children, people who have come from another galaxy to enlighten the humans. He says the star-children light up the earth with their magic and beauty but never quite belong here and often die young. He says that his best friend at school was a star-child. She drew beautiful and strange pictures then killed herself in her early twenties. He thinks that he and I are both star children too.

He starts taking ayahuasca. At first he goes to some town hall in an impoverished part of the city and takes the drug with fifteen other people. He is exhilarated: says that he has spoken to the dead, seen talking lights floating in the air.

Later he goes on a larger drug taking gathering in a field in the countryside. About a hundred people wear white and become intoxicated together. He does not feel properly welcome there and goes off this particular spiritual attempt.

The transvestite does not do anything for very long. He cannot bear disappointment or failure and abandons whatever he is attempting as soon as he has to face either. He numbs the pain by smoking pot, which makes him depressed and irritable.

This also goes for his worldly ambitions. He desperately wants to be a pop star. He dresses like one always and is certainly beautiful enough. He continually makes up tunes and sings them in a nasal voice as he wanders around the house. Does provocative little dances, making his face into a moue that he thinks is sexy. Shakes his slim hips like a girl.

Despite this, I think that he could be a pop star. I think that, if the world got the chance to look at him, then both women and men might fall for his liminal beauty. There are other boy-girls in the pop world who are less magical, less ethereal, less charming than he is.

A series of potential mentors slip through his life, exciting him wildly with their offers to manage him, put out a record, give him the key to the locked world of success. He is an innocent among wolves. Believes everything he is promised and sees fabulous futures sweeping before him. But he lacks the necessary ruthless self-confidence. He fails to thrust himself sufficiently far down the throat of anyone important enough to really send him stratospheric. And there are always little failures, little disappointments, each of which send him crashing into gloom and the awful marijuana. Then his life grinds to a halt for weeks and he snaps and growls at the boy and I as he stalks around the white bunker.

The transvestite's relationship with the boy is at first a mystery to me. The boy is very silent, gentle, almost somnambulant. He does very little with his life except work and exercise. He has a very beautiful body, lean and perfectly muscled, and a handsome, manly face.

He works as a flight attendant and is away at least half of the time, at work on flights to other countries. And when he is at home, we hardly notice him. Between trips to the gym he sits on the sofa and watches crap television. Whatever is on seems to keep him happy. He adores junk food and has a big plastic bottle of diet cola perpetually in his hand.

The transvestite does not think his boy is a star-child. He complains that he does not want to do anything, be anything, go anywhere. In turn, the boy says that he cannot bear the transvestite's dressing up. He hates the lipsticks and wigs and micro-mini skirts. And I am sure that he suffers horribly when the transvestite hits a low and is filthy to him.

Nonetheless, the logic of their relationship is quite clear. The transvestite knows that his nightlife is a transient place, where real friendship can't blossom amongst the eternal competition to be the most fabulous. And the boy also grew up on a farm, they are both farm boys at heart. The transvestite needs ballast and the boy provides it – ballast; roots curling into some simple earth; solidity and kindness. Family.

What the boy gets I am not sure. But they are happy together sometimes, eat pizza and doughnuts on the sheepskin rug. The transvestite abandoning health for delicious trans fat and a shared sugar-rush ecstasy.

One night, the transvestite takes me to a real cross-dressers club. A club for the ordinary men who are compelled to dress as women, not the pretty gay boys who do so to get attention and fame. We do not belong here, are here as tourists, although the transvestite gets a frisson from pretending to belong to this more serious side of transexuality.

It is a tacky, subterranean nightclub full of a strange mix of unremarkable, apparently straight men and clumsy transvestites with poor fitting clothes and anxious faces. A few very normal looking women also lurk in the shadows.

The transvestite has been here before. He tells me that most of the ordinary looking men are here because they have a fetish about men dressed as women. They are straight men who want to have– or fantasize about having – sex with men dressed as women. And that the transvestites here are mostly straight men too. He tells me that the women in the shadows are probably their wives.

I immediately feel very strongly that I do not belong here, but then a small, dark man with a beard slips up to me and tries to start a conversation, offers to buy me a drink. He is not English. Some sort of Arab I think. I look at him sceptically and refuse to respond. He leers at me and says "come on Ladyboy, come with me" in a thick accent.

I dart into the Ladies' toilet to escape him, seething. It is full of transvestites reapplying their makeup. Without thinking, I wail a complaint about this offence to my femininity. They are solicitous:

"He must be mad darling."

"Nobody could mistake you for a bloke."

"You're obviously a girl. Don't let him get to you."

I am amazed by their generosity.

We spend the rest of the night dancing foolishly to stupid, wonderful pop music. The transvestite and his friends protect me from the small man with the beard. I am weirdly bruised by his mistake. Feel like my identity is as sea-changeable as that of the men that I am dancing with. And they understand and wrap themselves around me like the strangest imaginable safety blanket.

After the music finally stops, I wait, exhausted, for the transvestite to get our coats. A middle-aged woman comes up to me and starts a conversation. She looks even more drained than I feel. She tells me that the handbag that she is holding belongs to her husband. That he insists she comes with him to the club. He is too scared to come by himself.

After we leave the transvestite club, I assume the night is over. I am wrong. The transvestite has met up with some other drag queens – the glitterly, perfect kind, do it for fun and adoration kind – who arrived late at the club. They all want to go to a fetish place which is just around the corner. More sightseeing.

I am tired and daunted at the thought of more strange sex and desire, of what I think will be dirty and frightening. But the trannies wrap themselves around me protectively again, promise that I they will look after me. I am enjoying this unlikely group of bodyguards and I trust that they mean what they say, so I go with them.

The club is in three layers of basement. Each level is more dimly lit than the last. The transvestite tells me that there is a room on the bottom level where anything can happen. But it seems to me than anything can happen anywhere in this place. Even as we stand at the bar on the first level, waiting to buy a drink, an enormous black man swings on a canvas sling a few feet away from us, completely naked. He skin is so dark and glossy, his muscles so beautiful that it seems perfectly natural that he should be so. Then I see that his erect penis, impossibly long, is penetrating a curvaceous red head from behind, in and out as he swings.

Most of the people here are not naked but they dress in ways that expose one or more erogenous zone. They all have breasts or buttocks, pussies or cocks emphasised or on display. They have wrapped themselves in rubber or leather, and many wear studs –pointing outwards or some-times inwards, pressed against their skin. The studs that point inwards seem always to be sharp.

Some people crawl around on all fours, some wear collars and leads around their necks. Some have splayed themselves nakedly across old wooden barrels, while others are queuing up to whip them. Women and men sit like queens and kings on throne-like chairs, while others, pretending to be their subjects, crawl up to them and ask permission to lick and suck their genitals.

I am almost too exhausted to respond to anything that I see at this place. I do not find it erotic. There is something too blankly human about these bodies, these desires. Other than the magnificent black man, most of the flesh on offer is grey, lumpen, pouched, ordinary. Sexually, it leaves me cold. But I am impressed by these people who can promenade their bodies and their strange and particular desires with such confidence.

I break away from my protective huddle of transvestites and wander around. It is 3am now and I am in a daze. A man in rubber propositions me. He is polite. I politely refuse him. He instantly grins at me, apologizes and melts back into the crowd. This happens once or twice more, always with the same immediate acceptance of my decision. I realize that the rules here are that anyone can do anything, including doing nothing. That in order to do all this, allow people to expose themselves like this, this place needs firm rules that allows people to feel – to be – safe. I start to feel that these people do not just have confidence, they have grace.

We do not stay here long. We are just tourists, exhausted ones, and we leave the wild people to get on with their graceful, twisted and long night. As we leave, I get the sense that even the trannies – with their worldliness and their own permissive sexuality - have been impressed and a little awed by what we have seen.

But this is not what our life is like in the everyday. In the everyday, we move through the white flat in choreographed patterns, being kind to one another. I feel gently and firmly loved by the boys, and I love them back in the same way.

We are becoming family.

I tell them about everything that I do, think, feel. Frustrations, dreams, dilemmas, infections, enthusiasms, everything. They are unfailingly enthusiastic about me. Never judge. Fret when I am sad and rejoice when things go well.

I am maternal with them. I cajole the transvestite when he is absurd, challenge him when he gives up, scold him when he poisons himself with drugs or becomes a caricatured gay-boy after spending too much time with his more exaggeratedly camp friends. His own mother was never very interested in him and I think that because of this he responds very well to this attention. Listens to me. Allows me to confront him on deep and difficult matters. Whereas the boy and I just have a quiet respect for each other. He is too sensible to need to be mothered, has been well mothered himself. But we become allies when the transvestite is dreadful. And the rest of the time we just glow fondly together.

I am so happy that I want to bind us all together tighter. Want to decorate our home with beauty. Expand our family. The transvestite and I start talking about having a baby together. He longs for a baby and so do I. We are sure it would be a beautiful baby. The boy is not so sure though, does not think that he could be happy with a baby in the flat. And he will not countenance the idea that we might have sex to make the baby. I think a baby made without sex would be a sad thing.

We cannot quite resolve the baby issue. So I decide that we should fill the flat with more animals.

The parrots come first.

My mother, who knows that I have always longed for parrots, tells me of an old opera singer who has died leaving two orphaned African Greys. The first time I go to meet them, they are hiding in a cupboard and refuse to come out. The second time, they stare at me suspiciously. But they are beautiful.

We buy them an enormous, elaborate cage.

Pagoda-like, with ropes to clamber on and four different bowls for water and different kinds of food. It looks very fine in the vast white flat. We fill it with long twisting perches made from wind-blown branches that we find on the heath.

When I go to collect the parrots I find that it has been left to me to catch them. Al I have to do this with are some thick leather gloves and a towel. They are terrified and so am I. But I manage it, and we are all left undamaged. Then Charlie, the big male, whistles with pleasure to feel the sun on his back as he sits in his little cage on the lawn outside the dead opera singer's house.

When we get to the flat we leave them in their small, familiar travelling cage for a few days, so that they can get used to their new underground world. We talk to them lovingly and feed them passion-fruit because we have been told that this is their favourite fruit. Very soon they start to rock their heads and retch, making scratchy noises at the back of their throat. I am convinced that they are choking and panic, but I can't think of any way that I can help them.

Later I learn that the retching is love, a preparation to vomit into a baby-bird's mouth.

And that the scratchy noise is the parrot equivalent of a purr.

The opera singer also had a dachshund. The boy gets very excited and wants to adopt it, but it has already been given a home. He tells me that he has always longed for a dachshund. He becomes unusually animated.

The transvestite and I decide to buy him a puppy. We find a tiny sausage dog puppy, her black and chestnut coat mottled silver. When we hand her to the boy something shifts in him, permanently. He becomes softened and joyous.

But our domesticity does not wholly satisfy me. I am restless and I start hunting for men. I go by myself to dark wild places. Nightclubs with elegant moulding on the walls and cupids on the ceilings, where everyone dresses as if it were still the middle of the last century, where waists are nipped in and skirts flare, lips are red and men wear moustaches. In these places, I am kissed by cads who thrill me but I do not bother to take them home. I have seen them kiss too many other women before me.

Drinking dens, illegal speakeasies become popular. In one of them, I meet a tall bald fashion photographer and his small vivid friend. I am excited by the secrecy of the place, and by the glamour of the photographer's profession. I get very drunk and dance and do acrobatic displays, getting the men to hold me up as I do handstands. One of them drops me on my head, but I am too drunk to care.

I take them both back to the white flat and we go to bed. I think that it will be thrilling to have sex with them both at the same time but, when it comes to it, I am frightened. I cling on to the photographer, the one I like best. He is a gentle Scottish man who is engaged to be married to a girl from his home city. I do not know if he realizes that I am frightened, but he strokes me kindly and I feel safer.

When I tell my girlfriends what I have done, they are horrified and lecture me about putting myself in danger. When I tell the boys, they laugh and are proud. I am proud too. I think it has been a great adventure. I sleep off my hangover nested in the sheepskin rug, the puppy tucked under my arm and the parrots shrieking happily.

I go to another party at a dowdy *ersatz* gentle-
man's club in a part of town that I have never liked
because of its mix of pretentiousness and seedy
housing. I have gone to the party with a man who
is himself terribly pretentious. He suffers from
having a father who is much more successful than
he is and a few screws loose in his brain. He is an
avid collector of status symbols: those that you can
buy, and those that you can't. We had sex once
and, afterwards, he started gabbling wildly in baby
talk and then cried. I found this revolting, so we
are not at the party as an item. But he is a good
hunting partner – as hungry for action as I am.

Looking round at the party, at the intentionally
dusty chandelier and dreadful ornate wallpaper, at
girls in pearls and dreary evening dresses, I do not
think we will find anything worth hunting. But my
partner in crime and I get very drunk anyhow,
because there is nothing else to be done. We do
not want to admit defeat.

Late in the evening we find ourselves sitting on
a stage at the edge of the dance floor with a group
of men who seem as bored and abandoned as we
are. One of them is a large and pasty man. He is
not attractive, but somehow seems very alive.

Vivid. I ask him about himself. He tells me that he used to be a Royal Marine. I once read a book by an American Navy Seal, so I am vaguely aware of what this means and intrigued.

"Have you ever killed a man?"

"Why do you want to know?"

"I don't think I've ever met someone who has killed a man."

"I have killed, yes."

"How did you kill him?"

"Why the hell do you want to know *that?*"

"Because I'm interested in your work."

"I stabbed him with a bayonet."

I am impressed. I take him home with me to the basement. When he is naked, I see that his body is covered with roughly drawn amateur tattoos faded to beautiful pastel colours. He gives me a guided tour of the words and pictures – each from a different military adventure. He tells me that they are pale because he is having them gradually removed by laser. This makes me sad. I think they are very beautiful.

He is very uninhibited, very proud. I enjoy him and fall a little for him – or at least for the myths of his former life. He has many stories of wild army bonhomie, of the exhilaration of leading a small team of men into danger, of a padre who they all adored, whose approach to keeping their souls intact involved riding a motorbike and having more tattoos than anyone else in their squadron.

But now he is just a salaryman for a telephone company. A very successful, rich salaryman, as he tells me. He tells me proudly that all of the ex-officers from his battalion have done brilliantly as civilians. They run banks and amass millions. He too plans to amass millions. As always, I am drawn to the safety net that I think would come with a great deal of money.

But after a few nights tangling with his tattoos, he stops calling. He doesn't return my calls, doesn't bother to explain.

A few weeks later, the boys meet him at the penthouse apartment of a rich gay businessman. He is with another woman, who they say looks rather like me. They say that he looks uncomfortable to see them, which delights them. They hiss at him.

I become entranced by rock bands. I like the darkness and the sweat and the abandon. I like one band in particular, which is led by a pair of intense boys who get messed up on drugs and break up the band almost as soon as I start listening to them. They each start their own bands and I trawl around the city as avidly as a teenage fan, watching either of the new bands whenever I can.

The first time I go to one of these concerts, I have two tickets but decide to go alone. It feels thrilling, that at last I am strong enough to go where I want without fear, to wear tight black clothes and be alone in dark places. As I queue outside the concert venue, which is dingy and on the outskirts of a fashionably grim part of the city, a skinny boy with a mohawk starts working the line, asking if anyone has spare tickets. He says he is a friend of the band, that he should be on the guest list, but something has gone wrong.

He is charming and pretty and looks like an adventure, so I give him my spare ticket.

He is called Lucian. He says that he is one of the real fans. A real fan who knows all of the other real fans because they have all been following the original band since the beginning. Despite the Mohawk and black eyeliner, he is a gentlemanly escort. Buys me drinks and thanks me effusively for the tickets. He is articulate and polite.

Lucian introduces me the other real fans - young girls and boys dressed elegantly in tea-dresses and trilby hats. I feel as though I am floating through their world, not really there. Until the music starts and I throw myself to the front of the crowd, to the heart of the crush where I am a caught in wave upon wave of swaying, leaping flesh. The dance is a crowd-dance. We are all swept from side to side by it, our muscles tense as we push ourselves against each other to stay upright, then as the chorus builds we leap high and abandoned, grabbing strangers' shoulders to push ourselves higher and higher to the brilliant, insistent riffs.

The band finishes their set and I find Lucian again. He has not danced, has been lurking in the shadows at the back. He is excited and wants to take me backstage to meet the singer, the messy genius addicted singer. I think this is supposed to be my reward for having given him the ticket.

We find our way backstage – in this tiny venue

it is not very far away. But the singer has gone – all that is left are a few battered guitar cases and the drummer who looks tired. Lucian thinks that he has gone off to take drugs somewhere private, and makes some urgent phone calls trying to track him down. He gets nowhere and I feel disappointed.

But Lucian is so charming and I am so elated by the gig that it doesn't really matter. I ask where he is going and he tells me that he is going to walk into town to catch a bus. It is a warm night so I decide to walk with him.

As we walk, Lucian tells me about his life. He is an unemployed heroin addict. He lives with his mother in a council estate in the far south of the city. His stepfather is his heroin dealer. He and his stepfather are very good friends. His says his real father played guitar for a famous band. He has never met him but likes the band's music. Lucian also plays the guitar and writes songs. He has started several bands and wants me to listen to his music.

He has strong religious beliefs. He is a Satanist. He does not equate this with evil but with freedom from rules, anarchic rebellion, fallen angels. And with power. He clearly believes that worshiping Satan gives him strength.

He says he isn't bothered by his addiction. He hates coming down, but says the highs are worth it.

He is interested in my life. I tell him that I am trying to save the planet. He seems as excited by my seriousness as I am by his anarchy, which is easy to digest as he is so polite and charming.

When we get to the bus stop, we are both swaying with exhaustion. I trip over a cardboard box on the side of the road waiting to be collected by the rubbish trucks and he catches me. We almost kiss but both draw back. I do so because I think he is too young, not because of the drugs or the devil-worship. I don't know why he does. It is possible that I am too old.

I give Lucian my phone number and he calls me frequently, usually when he is coming down from a high. We talk as he shakes and eats ice-cream. He often calls in the middle of the night. If I am bored or lonely, I answer his calls. If I am too tired, I don't bother. He usually sounds urgent and a little desperate when he calls, but he never asks me for anything. We flirt with each other gently and I probe him about the addiction and the religion. He likes being probed. I think it is wildly funny to have a Satanist as a friend. And I like the pretence that he needs me. Although I am quite sure that he doesn't really need me, so I feel that I am free to just enjoy this strange contact without letting it trouble me.

We meet only one more time. I take him to see the band created by the other genius from the band that split. This makes it a matching pair with the concert at which I met him.

Before the gig we meet at a bar near the river and drink vodka. He seems exhausted and nervous and despite our late night phone calls has very little to say to me. I am excited about the gig and impatient with this quiet mood. Eventually he tells me that his girlfriend is going to be at the concert with another man, that they have had a row, that he is worried about her. I find this irritating. I am taking him to the concert and so I think he should be as charming as when we first met. I am also a little jealous of this other girl, this younger woman, although I know that I would not like to be 24 years old and going out with a heroin addict.

The concert venue is weird. A large room at the top of an academic building overlooking the river. We take a steel clad lift up five floors to get there. As the lift gets higher, we can hear the thudding of the support band. The lift doors open and the music hits us.

Lucian wants to go and hunt down his girl and I let him, relieved to be on my own again, ready to melt into the crowd. I buy more vodka as the support band finishes its set and start to push myself forward towards the stage. This is a slow process – at this gig the fans are sweatier and meatier than before, even more transfixed by anticipation. There are no trilbies and tea dresses here – just boys with long hair and tight t-shirts. It feels more like rock and roll.

Eventually I find myself a few feet away from the front of the stage. By now, I expect something to be happening, but the band fail to appear. I don't mind. Just being here is thrilling, being in this throng. And yet I also feel very still and calm. I have nowhere to go, nothing to do but wait, no one to concern myself with. I do not feel any need to worry about Lucian. He abandoned me and I am glad of it.

Two young white boys with bushy afros are standing next to me in the crowd. They look sweet and intelligent, and are shouting happily to one another over the recorded songs that are being played to keep us happy while we wait. We start to talk. They are brothers, 14 and 16 years old, and have travelled by themselves from a town a hundred miles away to come to the gig. They talk cleverly about why both the old band that split and this new band are so important for their generation. But as the wait gets longer, they start to worry about whether they will be able to catch the last train home. I wonder if I will have to rescue them.

After an hour of waiting a beautiful black man climbs on stage and the crowd roars. He laughs at them and puts a finger to his lips. The crowd continues to roar, then the roar breaks down into a chant. They are chanting his name. He keeps his finger at his lips and eventually we realize that he wants to speak to us, wants us to be still. We quieten and he reaches for the mike. Tells us that the lead singer, the genius, has a migraine.

We moan. But he says that they are desperate to play to us, that they will try to once his painkillers start working. We cheer wildly.

And the wait continues.

Then finally a technician comes onto the stage and taps the mike, one-twos. The black man comes back, this time with drumsticks in his hands, stands behind the drum-kit and starts drumming a powerful beat. And suddenly the band are all there, slouchy and magnificent, shoulders slumped and hair a mess and they turn to the drummer, lift their guitars sky-high, and on his beat crash into the first song.

The wall of flesh this time is almost suffocating, almost brings me down as it surges forward. But I remember how to flow with it and just let go, let myself push, leap, sway with it. This music is incredible, fast and furious and yet delicate. It tells us to be wild and beautiful and free. Happy and sad. But most of all it tells us to be a frenzied pack. A delirious, frenzied pack. I am so glad to be buried in the heart of this pack. I do not think I ever have been so content. Wildly content.

In the middle of it all, a young blonde boy starts dancing with me, manages to take my hand in his, put his hand on my waist as if we were in a ballroom. He whirls me around violently and I whirl him back so we accelerate in our spin and crash back into the rest of the crowd laughing madly. He grabs me and kisses me briefly, but I break away and plunge back through the wall of men.

I wish it would never end.

But it does of course. The band let us down softly with a gentle ballad played on two acoustic guitars and then melt from the stage. The lights come up and we rub our eyes and hobble towards the exits. The blonde boy finds me and we grin at each other. He asks for my phone number.

Lucian has disappeared and I have lost my cell-phone in the crush. I walk home along the river. The night air is sweet and cool.

There is a little man who has just broken up with his girlfriend. Another singer, but neither as mad or beautiful as mine, although this one was once briefly famous. He is watching football with one of my friends in an anonymous, tedious pub in the middle of the city. I am feeling provocative so I'm wearing a t-shirt made of translucent black silk. Translucent enough to show my underwear and the shadow of my navel. We watch the game and our team loses so we all go back to my friend's flat and get drunk and then it is so late that we fall asleep in a pile like dissolute puppies.

I wake up in the middle of the night feeling nauseous and see that he is sitting on the edge of my friend's bed, head in his hands.

"I don't know what to do," he whispers.

"About what?"

"About my girlfriend."

"Then why don't you try kissing me?"

He does, a small hard ecstatic kiss. I am surprised by how it feels.

In the morning, he is anxious. He wants my phone number but is also frightened that his girlfriend will find out that he has kissed me. I find his fear pathetic and insulting, but the kiss was compelling so I give him my number anyway.

When he calls, all he wants to do is talk about the songs he is writing. I find this exhausting and do not want to help. He is only interested in himself and his songs and whether he is going to manage to become famous again. I am silent as he delivers a long monologue throughout which I strain to hear a note of interest in me. None sounds. Only the memory of the small kiss keeps me listening, impatiently listening for some hint that it might be repeated.

Eventually the monologue peters out.

"So do you want to see me again?"

He hums and haws and says he is not sure, that he must consider the ex-girlfriend's feelings.

I hang up and feel furious that I've wasted time on him. Moments later, he calls back and he invites me to another city to watch him play. I didn't know that he lived somewhere else.

The air is shockingly cold as I get off the train. It feels strange to arrive in an unknown city so late in the evening. I am wearing silky black cigarette pants that fit close to the skin and the ice wind slaps at my legs. I have painted my face on the train and wear dark lipstick, slashes of black and gold across each eyelid. War paint for entering enemy territory.

I feel exposed to the wind and the strangeness of the city so I hail a warm cab to take me to the gig. It is only a five minute ride. This is a much smaller city than I'm used to. It feels emptier and colder and neater than the capital.

Pushing my way through the doors into the unknown venue gives me a greater thrill than usual. I am excited because I know that I may fuck the singer after the gig, but I also feel, even more than usual, the song of the solitary hunter in my blood. I push to the bar and buy myself a double vodka and tonic. All the barmen and most of the other men in the small venue have thick beards on their faces that give them a false maturity but also make them look softer than the men I am used to seeing. I feel excellently anonymous as I look around at them from behind my makeup.

I do not plan to speak to the small singer until after his set, but he sees me and comes over. I offer to buy him a drink and he says he doesn't need one as he gets his free all night because he is singing. He is wired and nervous and distant. I know this pre-performance mood, I've seen it before, so I am quiet and still and do not ask for his attention. I doubt that he will notice my tact.

He goes off to talk to his band – a complicated ensemble of violinists and drummers and keyboard players. I drink more and lean on the bar and enjoy being silent and alone in the noise and smoke. The venue is about half full, which is a decent turn-out for a new act. I am pleased for him, start feeling invested in his success despite my determination to remain detached, as detached as he is from me.

When the music starts, it is soulless and beautiful and his voice sounds otherworldly. Small, strange, empty and mildly threatening. The words full of tangled anger and desire.

After the set he is still anxious and even more wired. When he comes off stage, I stay by the bar and enjoy my vodka buzz as he talks to the music business people that he needs to impress. In a while he comes over to me and takes me backstage, briefly stroking the small of my back as we walk.

The backstage space is white walled and harshly lit. I talk to his pretty girl violinists who are young music students from the university. They are sweet and a little vacuous, despite their virtuosity. But I am patient, humming with vodka and curious to see what happens next. The instruments are wrapped in their cases and we go out into the cold air to look for somewhere else to drink. He does not invite me to go with them, but he seems to assume that I will.

After a long walk through bitter cold, we end up at a narrow, scruffy bar where he knows the barmen and most of the punters. It is my sort of place. Good music, a mixed crowd, friendly. Everyone so off their faces and Northern that I feel welcomed and warm for the first time this evening. I pretend to ignore him and set to drinking and talking, but my skin crackles, waiting for him to touch me.

Later still we are in a taxi on the way to his flat in the outskirts of the city. We are impossibly drunk and we still haven't kissed.

He takes me into his small basement flat and we fall into his bed, which has damp sheets, and finally he leans over and kisses me, a small, hard kiss again and our bodies dance together beautifully.

Three hours later he wakes up in the throws of a diabetic crisis from all the alcohol. He can't find his insulin, stumbles around his flat swearing as he looks for it. I follow him around the tiny flat but can't help him. He nearly faints before he finds the drugs. Then he injects himself but overdoses because he is drunk and starts shaking. He crams chocolate into his mouth to get his blood sugar balanced.

I still feel drunk and turned on and half asleep and the medical crisis seems too bright and real. But I sit at the kitchen table and enjoy the sight of the hypodermic needles going into his arm.

When we wake up again it is lunchtime and he cooks me breakfast. He doesn't seem to want to look at me. After we eat he takes me into his living room and plays me music for a few hours until it is time for him to drive me to catch my train. He shows no interest in me but he still wants me to comment on his music, to care about it. I am waiting for him to kiss me again, but he doesn't. Instead, he plays me a song that he didn't play at the gig, a duet with a Swedish girl that he is excited about. It is supposed to be dark but I find it a bit absurd.

On the train home, I feel incredibly empty.

He calls me again after a week or so and talks to me about his music. I answer automatically. He says he has another gig coming up, at the same venue in his city. He does not invite me to come.

But I am bored and I can't believe how amazing fucking him felt so I decide to go anyway.

Again the cold air slaps me as I get out of the train. This time I know where I'm going so I walk to the gig. He sees me and comes over.

"I thought you would come."

"Do you mind?"

"No. Not really. Do you have anywhere to stay?"

"No."

He looks at me coldly and I meet his look, keeping still and silent behind my makeup.

His performance is exactly the same as it was at the last gig. Polished, self contained and absent. Afterwards we go to the same narrow scruffy bar, and this time I get even drunker. I love the bar. Everyone is as pissed as I am and they don't care why I'm there.

A DJ is playing at the bar and I dance with a girl with bleached blonde hair. She is as drunk as me and I think she's great. We twirl each other around and grind our asses together and laugh when we fall over. The other people at the bar mostly ignore us but when we fall, they try and catch us and don't seem to mind even when we spill their drinks.

I feel vengeful towards the small singer. I feel that he owes me something, owes me some fucking affection. I tell the slutty blonde this. She agrees with me enthusiastically. But even though I'm this drunk, I don't expect to get what I'm owed, so I mostly ignore him and continue to dance and laugh and fall over.

When I do look over at him he is talking quietly to his band. He looks even smaller than usual, and slightly harried. This pleases me.

By closing time, I have stopped drinking and started to sober up. I know that it is 3am and that I am in a city where I know no-one except the small singer. I wonder if the bleach blonde will give me a bed.

But the singer comes up to me as I stand wondering.

"Let's go," he says.

The cold air sobers me up even more. I feel alert, like a fox. I have fox eyes and can see in the dark, a fox's nose and I can smell my prey. But I am softened by his taking me home, as though this is a tender act.

When we get to his basement he takes a mirror off the kitchen wall and uses a library card to cut four fat lines of coke. He rolls a ten-pound note and passes it to me first. More tenderness.

He is looking at me now, steadily, as though he is evaluating what he has brought home with him. I hold his gaze, still protected by the makeup, then I lean over and sniff up the white powder. It is good and my gums and lips are quickly numb. He snorts his in an elegant swipe, practiced. I admire the movement. Then we stand steadily face to face, our heads nearly touching the low ceiling, knees loose, hands behind our sides, as if we might start a fight.

Then the drug reminds us of the joy of our previous fucking and we go to bed.

This time, we cannot sleep afterwards but laugh wildly, amazed by how good it feels. A perfect animal act. Some ideal locking on of pheromones and angles.

In the morning he is affectionless again and talks only of his music. He has some new songs that he has been writing with a Swedish producer which he plays me, pumping me for a response. I say a few things but I can't feel my way into his icy music.

He is cold, but I cannot believe that he won't want to fuck again, it was so extraordinary. I suggest staying another night.

"No. I think it would be better if you go home."

He drives me to a station out of town. Drops me off with half an hour to wait until the next train. A sharp wind is blowing drizzle vertically across the platform. I am furiously hungry so I walk to a drive-by McDonalds half a mile from the station and try to buy something wholesome to eat.

After eating, I still feel ravenous.

I don't hear from him again for a few weeks, then a CD arrives in the post with a single track on it. It is a new track, but I recognize the style of the Swedish producer. The track hums and whines and quavers around an erotic obsession. I do not like it, but I listen to the words avidly. They are about kissing in a cold darkness, a woman with makeup like a mask, sex without words. It must be about me.

I assume that this is the only way that he can express his desire. I play it to the transvestite, who is impressed by the track and delighted to be living with a muse. Then I listen to it over and over again by myself, lying on the golden bed, replaying in my head what I can remember of the sex.

Then he calls me and asks me what I think of it, and during the conversation it becomes clear that the song is about another woman, a singer, some blonde he has worked with once. I realize that he only sent me the song because he is desperate for an audience and knew I would listen to it.

I tell him that I think it is meaningless.

I only see him once again. He and his band and the Swedish woman are playing in a small but influential venue in the middle of my city. He wants to impress some record company people and needs an enthusiastic audience so he calls me and asks me to come. I go with our mutual friend. I have been to this place before, when I managed the Singer.

We watch the performance which is as polished as usual, although I think that tonight I can detect a hint of nervousness in his tight little face. The stakes are higher here than when he played in Liverpool. The blonde looks slightly tacky – bleach blonde with heavy black eyeliner, a little messy and smudged. It looks OK when she's on stage but, after the performance, as we all stand together in an uneasy circle near the bar, it just looks dirty.

In the circle, my friend and I laugh and flirt with one another, as we always do. We make filthy small talk. I joke about the size of my friend's cock. The bleach blonde laughs and the small singer looks even more tense.

We leave the two of them alone and go and sit at the back of the venue and laugh more. Being near the small singer and knowing that I will not end up having sex with him makes me feel irritable. But I am drinking and in good company and can feel a growing sense of liberation. I won't get to fuck him, but neither will I have to wake up alongside his bewildering indifference.

Everyone gets drunker. The small singer and the blonde sit at a table a few metres away from us. We can't hear what they are saying. She sits upright, her face blank, while he is hunched up opposite her, leaning forward over the table, his face hidden from us, leaning in towards her breasts. When we look over again, the blonde has left but he is still in the same position, leaning in towards the space that she has left behind her. A few moments later he turns slowly to look at me, his eyes burning.

After the venue closes we walk through Soho looking for somewhere that is still serving alcohol, the small singer and I, our mutual friend and a few other hangers on. As usual the streets here are weirdly, hustlingly busy for the early hours of the morning. The small singer is silent but we don't really notice. We are only interested in our hunt for early morning booze.

We find a place that will serve us, a quasi-nightclub with huge blue velvet sofas and dim light coming from faux crystal chandeliers. Our little group collapses itself onto one of the sofas. I am sitting between the small singer and our mutual friend. I order a bottle of champagne because I feel sick and want something light and dry in my stomach. Bad pop music is playing loudly. Too loudly for conversation but after a few minutes the small singer turns to me anyhow and spits

"How could you do that to me?"

"Do what?"

"Make me look ridiculous in front of her."

"But I didn't."

"You did. Everything is ruined."

I have no idea what he is talking about, but I can see that he is furious. He leans back on the sofa like a cobra waiting to strike, and I flinch despite myself.

"You bitch. You told her that I had a small cock."

I laugh helplessly.

"But I only said that his" – I pat our mutual friend on the knee – "was huge."

"Because you wanted her to fuck him not me, you stupid jealous bitch." He is really hissing now and I think he would like to hit me. "Because you want to keep me for yourself."

I try to keep my voice calm. "I promise you that I don't".

He pauses at this, rocks back into the blue velvet, and I realise that he is very, very drunk. He rocks a little more, then manages to stand up. He stands unsteadily, then turns, leans forward and puts his hands on my shoulders as if he is going to kiss me. But instead he throws me back against soft blue velvet cushions, pushes his hard little forehead into mine and screams into my face

"I should never have touched you. You are a sick cunt. I hate you. Keep away from me you sick man-eating cunt. I'm not scared of you. Keep away. Keep away or I swear I'll fucking kill you."

This goes on for a few minutes and his voice becomes so twisted that I can barely make out the words.

And then he leaves and, afterwards, I feel shocked and nauseous and shivery, as if I really have been hit.

But our mutual friend puts a long reassuring arm around me and we finish the champagne. And then I realise that there is another man with us, a friend of the small singer's, who has long hair and a beautiful face and a gentle voice and he is also kind and reassuring and so I take him home with me back to the cool basement where we lie on the long soft black calfskin sofa together and watch the light creep back into the early morning sky.

We kiss a little, but we don't fuck.

Rotting Man

I become lonely. I lie on the gold bed in my damp basement and cringe with loneliness. The boys try to keep me happy – the transvestite plays me vaguely spiritual music and massages my back and his boy lets me use the dachshund as a hot water bottle – but being alone nags at me like a rotten tooth. The absence of someone is sending me mad. I want to howl at the moon and go hunting.

No-name writes a review of me for a dating website. Becomes my cyber-pander. His review says: "She is beautiful, strong, clever and funny. I think this is a very rare combination. You should try and meet her." I add a picture of myself wearing the vintage tutu with the female rabbit on my lap. We both look radiant and slightly unreal.

I spend days scrolling through the men who are advertising themselves, searching for something that will set one out against the others. It is exciting to be able to secretly examine them, to try and extrapolate some truth from the lies that they tell about themselves, that we are all telling about ourselves. Trying to peer behind their digital masks.

Many of the men are looking for women at least a decade younger than themselves. This revolts me.

Men start to contact me. A dentist from the north is very insistent and, when I say that he is too far away to make it worth meeting, he tells me about his expensive cars as if this must change my mind. Others are more tentative, as if they are not quite convinced that they want to meet me.

I decide to ignore all of the men who contact me. I want to be on the front foot. On the offensive.

So I choose a man who looks pretty in his picture, which is black and white with deep shadows. He claims to be a scriptwriter and looks cooler than the other men on the website, as if he might belong in a rock band. In the flesh he is small and unremarkable. We meet late at night in a bar above an underground station. Large semi-circular windows allow in geometric arches of street-light. The windows are more interesting than the man, who is neurotic and incredibly self-absorbed. But we get drunk together and I am so desperate to get to the end of my search that I kiss him though I do not let him walk me home. I can tell that he is excited about me so, the next day, I have to call him and tell him not to be.

I keep scrolling and imagining. For each man that interests me a little, I tell myself a story about a future. A future of domesticity, or wealth, or adventure, depending on what digital mask the man is wearing.

Then I find a man who intrigues me. His friends have written an essay about him and he sounds clever and funny. Just as I am about to mail him, he contacts me spontaneously. I find the coincidence exciting and think it must be meaningful.

We meet in a secret private club that is hidden underground, beneath one of the theatres in the centre of the city. A scruffy, cheap place where it seems wild things could easily happen. Scruffy enough that it wouldn't matter what happened, what got spilt or broken.

I recognise him from his photograph before he sees me. He is sitting upright and alert, reading from a pile of newspapers that spill over the table he sits at towards the back of the place. He is a largish man, with short fine hair in tufts somewhere between messy and fashionable. He wears voluminous clothes in dark colours, under which he is definitely not slim, though I do not think he is fat either. The most remarkable thing about him is the colour of his skin. It has an extraordinary pallor –a yellow grey, something like the colour of moonlit squirrel fur. Skin that the sun hasn't touched for a long time.

I do not find him unattractive, so I go over.

"Hello."

He looks up and his face cracks into a toothy grin. His teeth are also yellow grey.

"Hello, you."

And immediately I feel invaded, though not unpleasantly. There is something unquiet about this "you", something restless that I can feel wants to burst its banks. I decide that I should stay very still and watch him.

"Can I get you a drink? Do you like this place? Did you even know it existed?"

"I like it very much. Thank you for bringing me. It's exactly my kind of place."

And I am grateful. It is as if in bringing me here he has already given me an exotic present, one that I actually like. The rarest kind of present. I can't resist grinning.

I start feeling drawn to him. We start drinking and telling our stories.

We both have grandiose stories to tell. I tell him that I work with pop stars, indulging them so that they can help me to save the planet, rubbing myself in their glamour so that I can feel beautiful. He tells me that he casts actors in films, spends his days at auditions and nights in bars and clubs hunting for a glimmer of magic that he can sell to millions. He has had great success but then he crashed and burned and now he has nothing.

But originally he was a journalist. A local newshound. He waxes lyrical about this work. I tell him that I have little respect for journalists, cannot see the point in describing things without intervening in them, or in telling stories that are true. He laughs, a high pitched hyena laugh, and tells me that I am wrong, that good journalists do intervene.

"And are you a good journalist?"

"I once was. I got sidetracked."

"Will you ever get back on track?"

"I might, if the right conditions materialise."

"What conditions?"

"A strong wind in the right direction might do it."

"I see."

And I do. Here is someone who needs to be blown away from his past to crash into some better future.

We kiss before we leave the bar.

I take him home with me, to the cool white basement, because he doesn't have anywhere to take me to. He has been sleeping on friends' floors. He seems enthusiastic about me, but also slightly aloof. I can see that he needs to hold himself up, prop himself up, with memories of who he has been previously, in order to maintain a centre of gravity. Otherwise he might whirl away in the four winds.

That night he lies beside me on the golden bed and wheezes. He is asthmatic and the basement is poisonous to him – feathers and fur and mould on the walls from the damp. But he doesn't seem to mind the wheezing, and the feeling of his soft, bulky arm under the curve of my neck is comforting. I am glad not to be alone.

"I'm sorry that this place makes you wheeze."

"Don't be sorry. It's good to be surrounded by animals. I love dogs. And I like being underground too. It feels reassuring."

His skin looks grey-green even in the dim light from the nightlight that another lover gave me to scare away the deep darkness that used to frighten me. Skin like this suits being underground.

He hauls himself up and over me and I feel slightly suffocated by his fleshy weight but I abandon myself to the suffocation and take it as something erotic.

Neither of us can breathe.

He has nowhere to go, so I invite him to stay. For a few days I think, though at the same time I am already thinking until you are healed and strong and back on your feet. It does not occur to me to consult the boys about this. I just tell them that he is staying for a while. The transvestite is pleased because he thinks that the grey man could help him become an actor, but the boy says nothing and seems a little tense.

Sunday comes and the grey man and I go to the flower market to the east of the city and he buys me white roses that I like because they are glamorous, though I am sad that they have no fragrance. Then we go and eat a richly greasy breakfast in an old Italian café, after which we need to walk off our food coma so find ourselves wandering around the area. After a while he stops and says:"I used to live here. My flat was just over there. I used to park my car just here. Come with me and I'll show you."

The flat is in a faceless gated development, which comprises a row of ugly new brick houses and a feeble water feature in a communal garden. We follow a woman with a bicycle in through the gates and he points out the windows of his old flat which are at ground floor level. We sit on a concrete bench set in some dry white gravel beside the water feature.

"I miss my car."

"What happened to it?"

"I had debts. The taxman forced me to sell it."

"And the flat?"

"The same. I had to sell everything. But I didn't mind losing the flat. I hated it by then."

Then, as we stay sitting on the concrete bench getting colder and colder, he tells me an appalling story about what happened to him in the flat. It is so awful that I cannot repeat it. I am deeply disturbed, but feel sympathy for this broken man. I want to help.

I tell him that he can stay with me for a while. Move in properly. He says he will if I let him buy me a TV for the bedroom. He wants one with a built-in DVD player so that he can watch porn. He says he'd like us to watch porn together. He buys the TV online, plus a feather-free duvet and pillows in what seems to me to be a rather futile attempt to keep his asthma in check. He wheezing is getting worse and he finds it hard to walk up the steep hill to the flat. Whenever he gets back from a trip to the city he goes to bed to recover from the effort.

He is very excited when the TV arrives and wants to go out that night to the red light district to buy porn and trashy lingerie. I have always found porn upsetting, so I resist.

"But I don't like porn."

"Everyone likes porn."

"I find it upsetting."

"Why, because it turns you on too much? Don't you like being turned on?"

"Of course I do. By another human being."

"They are human beings."

"They're human beings pretending to be cartoons."

"Sexy cartoons though."

"Too sexy. It's unreal. And the women are pretending to be objects."

"Not all the women."

I raise my eyebrows at him

"We'll find some porn where the women are in control. Beautiful and in control. Would you like that?"

"Maybe."

We head off into a November night, wrapped in padded coats, scarves wound round our necks, hats pulled down over our ears. He is very pleased to have won the battle and keeps grinning at me over his scarf. The tube tunnels us into the heart of the city, right in the middle, to a classy sex shop with sleek black mirrored windows.

I have never been to a sex shop before, so I am curious. Inside the shop seems bland and over-lit, nothing hidden or enticing. But the grey man is little-boy-excited, almost hopping with joy as he shows me round, cooing over nurses outfits and crotchless underwear. I can see that it is going to be easy to please this one, though I tell him that I won't wear any of the cheap trash in the shop. So he takes me to look at the porn DVDs, flicking through them confidently, pointing out the ones that he likes best. On the covers the women have enormous, pendulous breasts hanging over tiny hips, their thighs spread at strangely elegant angles. He tries to get me involved in choosing some to buy. I find it hard to concentrate, but in the end we find a few where the women look like they might be powerful but not violent or masochistic and I reluctantly agree to their purchase.

Then we leave the shop and dive back into the cold air then and he drags me up an alleyway. He is walking surprisingly fast and his wheezing accelerates. His strange skin is slightly luminous in the streetlight and he has a twisted little half smile on his face.

"Where are we going now?"

"I'm taking you somewhere you'll like better than that place."

"How do you know?"

"Because you like beautiful things."

The shop has ornate moulding around the window, painted glossy vulva red. In the window angular, beautiful mannequins with pillar-box lips and sharp black bobs look aggressively out at the street, pushing their neat breasts forward at us and a few passers by in the tiny alley. The lingerie that they wear is ornate and exquisite, jewel coloured, tasselled, ribboned and velveted. Beautiful first, seemingly provocative only as an afterthought.

He pauses outside the shop and I think that perhaps he has only brought me here to look. Then he says "you go in", and I say "won't you come with me?", and he says "I don't know if I can bear to."

"Why not?"

"It's all too wonderful. Too much for me. You go in and choose something and then I'll come in afterwards and pay."

"No, that's too weird. I'm not going in without you."

So he trails in after me and lurks nervously as I examine the racks of ribbon and mesh and velvet. Occasionally he darts forward to look closely at what I'm looking at, and sometimes he murmurs warmly. He behaves as if we are on holy ground, as if the frills and slits and ruffles are made of hot holy iron that will sear him if he gets too close.

I cannot bring myself to choose from the purely dysfunctional, the knickers with thick lines of marabou along their margins, bustiers designed to reveal three-quarters of the nipple, g-strings with slashed crotches, waist cinches designed to stop your breath. These are the things that he murmurs most intensely over and I can see their beauty, but they are too much for me.

Instead, I choose simplicity. Black silk. A bra that I know my breasts will spill up and out of and black silk knickers that tie at the side with enormous, enticing bows. I can imagine enjoying having these bows pulled open.

I try the silky things on in a cubicle lined with red velvet, behind curtains of more red velvet, so heavy that they could suffocate one. A girl in teetering heels and a cartoonishly curvy uniform fusses over me, checking that my flesh is correctly constrained and revealed. I stick my head through the thick red curtains and try to call the grey man into the velvet box to inspect the wares, but he shakes his head vigorously, like a little boy refusing something healthy to eat.

Once I am cinched in, I look at myself in the mirror. The lighting in the velvet box is soft and in it the black silk looks like a shadow, an absence, a slash of night against my bone white skin.

The teetering assistant parts the velvet a little and thrusts some more black ribbon through the gap. "He wants you to have this." It is a suspender belt. I have always hated suspender belts as my hips are narrow and they tend to slip down them. However. this one is beautifully contoured and inviting so I try it and the pair of fishnet stockings that the cartoon assistant also thrusts through to me and when I am finished I see that I am trussed up, slashes of silk and stocking criss-crossing my flesh, revealing and concealing, tying me up and inviting another to open me.

The silky black things are wrapped in pink tissue and plunged into pink boxes and tied up with broad pink ribbons and put into a glossy pink cardboard bag with pink ribbon handles and he gets out his credit card and pays hundreds and hundreds of pounds for them.

We are both silent on the way home, the cold and the hill catching our breath.

We do not unpack the pink boxes that night, nor do we watch the DVDs. We are tired and he says that he wants the first wearing, the first watching, to be a special, prepared for event. A day or so later, I come home from work to find the bed messed up and the DVDs and their cases spread across it. I do not want to imagine his day.

But the boxes are still pristine.

He seems to get a thrill from anticipating my wearing the lingerie and wants to linger over it. So the boxes stay in the corner of the damp white underground bedroom for a few weeks. Then, one weekend, he goes out during the day, which is unusual, and then calls me while he is out and tells me that he has champagne and cocaine and that he wants me to ask the boys to go out and leave us alone. Luckily I do not have to – the transvestite is

DJ-ing at some hot new club and the boy is on a flight to Casablanca. Lucky because I cannot imagine telling them to go out so that I can have sex with the grey man. I do not think that they like him.

I know that he has bought the champagne and drugs to celebrate the first wearing of the lingerie. I am glad because I know that they will numb me to my lack of feeling for him and make it easier to be a beribboned slut. I turn the heating up in the flat and wash myself and dry my hair carefully, trim and pluck my pubic hair so that it won't sprout out around the silk. I think that trimmed, plucked pubic hair is eerily childlike but I know that it is required, it is how the polished porn girls do it. I would prefer to have a bush exploding between my legs, hanging down.

I have bought the transvestite a picture of one of his favourite female pop stars naked standing beside an American freeway with pubic hair like that and it thrills me. The picture sits in the kitchen propped on the top the tumble dryer. "Super hot," says the transvestite. The women in the line drawings in my parent's seventies edition of *The Joy of Sex* are also wonderfully hairy as they twist themselves into their serious poses.

But I make myself neat and then dry my hair and give it silky curls and then I oil myself all over and sit naked on the bed looking at the boxes, waiting for the oil to sink in so that it doesn't stain the silk. It seems wrong to open the boxes without the grey man, but I know that he will want me to be wearing the stuff by the time he gets home. So I pull open the ribbons and enjoy the way that they slither off the glossy boxes, the way the box opens to reveal the pink tissue, the way the pink tissue rustles as it reveals the black silk. I stroke it and think that this opening is probably the greatest pleasure that I will get from these things.

I wish I already had champagne in my stomach and cocaine up my nose. It doesn't seem right to put the silk on sober.

By the time he comes home, I'm wearing a short skirt and a silk shirt over the trussing. I can feel the bra like a metal band around my ribs. The constraint makes me panicky and I want to breathe deeply to diffuse the panic but of course I can't because the bra stops me. He comes in, wheezing as ever, and collapses on the buttery black leather of the long sofa. He doesn't look comfortable. Nobody ever does on this sofa, a piece of furniture that seems to be designed to make you slither to the floor. But he seems strangely at ease with being uncomfortable, as if it is his natural state.

The cold and the hill have not brought a flush to his grey cheeks but his eyes are bright.

"You look beautiful."

"Thank you."

"I'm not going to ask what you are wearing under that."

"No, please don't. It is a secret."

He laughs, pleased that I am playing with him.

"Take this and put it in the freezer. It should chill quickly, it's bone cold outside. Then let me catch my breath a little darling."

"Yes, darling."

I take the champagne to the freezer wishing that it were cold enough to drink immediately. Luckily there is a bottle of expensive designer vodka already waiting in the ice, so I take a slug and feel it run down my throat, viscous with the cold but still burning me.

Then I sit on the steps beside the parrots and listen as his wheezes start to slow. The two grey birds watch me curiously, the female wondering as ever whether I'll come close enough for her to bite a chunk of my flesh, the male scratching his throat and bobbing lovingly.

He is a very gentle, beautiful bird and, as the vodka makes its way through the lining of my stomach, I wish that I could have him on my shoulder, have both of them on my shoulders, one to rub his head against my ear and the other to tear out the flesh of anyone who comes near.

The wheezing ends and his breath only has a slight catch in it. I take the champagne to him poured into two beautiful engraved glasses that I gave the transvestite and his boy one valentine, so delicate that they seem almost as light as air. I kneel on the sheepskin and enjoy its softness. I would quite like to curl up on it now and sleep.

He sits on the calfskin sofa, still looking uncomfortable, but his gaze is steady as he raises his glass to me and I raise mine to him. I am grateful for its numbing dryness.

After a while, he heaves himself up and puts a CD on the stereo. Anew band that one of the actors he discovered sings in. I have tried to tell him what I think about their songs, but he isn't interested in my opinion. He doesn't like the music I like and doesn't think that I know anything about music so I have stopped listening to any music at all.

Once the music is playing, he walks over to the far wall and lifts a picture off the wall, sits down again on the calfskin and puts it on his lap. He pulls out a wrap of cocaine and a razor blade and starts chopping. The picture is a delicate print from a book called *The Childhood of Peter Pan*. In the picture, exquisite little fairies in dresses made of petals and leaves are dancing on cobwebs. I try not to look at them as I take the rolled up twenty from him and snort up two lines.

Once we are drunk and wired, and I am even more numb, we go to the damp bedroom and light candles and he leans across the bed and puts one of the porn DVDs into the DVD player and I watch as the thighs in elegant angles come to life, girls in fantasy sets, leaning back on sweeping staircases in Californian mansions, tanned thighs against white marble steps, rubbing their bare pussies and licking their glossy lips. We lie side by side watching, but pretty soon he reaches for me and unbuttons me and pulls me on top of him and I close my eyes and feel him brush against the silk, which he pushes past but doesn't undo, until he comes. He has viscous, weird smelling come that is the thing I like least about him.

The wheezing worsens and the grey man starts spending more and more time in bed. I go out to work every day, but the boys give me updates on him when I get home, telling me whether or not he has left my room, the house, whether he has eaten anything, what he has broken that day. He is clumsy and thoughtless and quickly works his way through much of our china.

He also drops my brand-new Apple laptop, leaving a permanent dent in the lid which stops it closing properly. I assume he's dropped it in the throes of some masturbatory ecstasy inspired by the online porn that he watches almost constantly. I know that he does because he tells me about it, the second report about his day that I get every evening – his about what he has found to be furious about or wank over online, the boys' about his movements in the flat.

Every night the boys roll their eyes and tell me that he is weird and that they don't know why I am with him. I don't have a good answer for them, but I ask them to be patient. I am starting to tell myself that he is only here because he has nowhere else to go, that to turn him out now would be a cruelty.

By the time I get home to these reports every evening, my room feels fetid. The sheets are crumpled and smell of sweat and wanking and coffee. I feel sad about my beautiful sheets, which are pale grey and covered with enormous beautiful delicate orchids. They are increasingly stained, and the patch on which he sits slumped in bed, hunched over my computer, is wearing thin. Everything else in the room is also in disarray – shoals of dishevelled clothes, dirty plates, crumpled newspapers swim across the floor revoltingly mixed in with the white dust from the crumbling plaster on the walls.

In the evenings, he is usually watching appalling TV – mindless game shows and American crime dramas. He only talks to me in the ad breaks.

I try to be charming and kind and playful with him and I cook him good food that he eats unwillingly. I want him to feel happy and strong.

Strong enough to get out of bed and make himself a life again. Strong enough to get out of bed, pack his bags and leave. But the flat and the animals are steadily poisoning him and he only gets iller and more sedentary.

It is my birthday, so I must of course throw a party. This time I decide that everybody must dress as animals. I have my hairdresser put my hair up in pretty coils that I thread with the boy parrot's most beautiful cast-off feathers. They are grey with vermillion tips. My grey silk dress is also feathered with marabou at the hem.

I buy the grey man grey squirrel's ears and a grey squirrel's tail and force him to wear them. He does so, even though it looks absurd, because he wants to indulge me. He still calls me darling all the time and paws at me affectionately with his clammy hands. I have started to find him revolting but I hide it, putting on a mask of enthusiasm, trying to be his cheerleader.

Just before the party starts, I notice that the worn patch on my beautiful delicate sheets has a tear in it.

The party is not a success. Although it looks like a success. The guests come as foxes and hounds, sleek black cats, an armour plated armadillo. One guest wears an elegant, sky scraping giraffe hat that grazes our high white ceiling and nearly gets tangled in the LED lights that we have strung across it. Another has glued feathers to the skin of her arms and legs and has peacock plumes bursting from her knickers and headdress. A man stoops under the weight of a real polar bear skin, so vast and heavy that it drags on the floor and forces him to lumber rather than dance, just as a real bear might. Another man wears nothing but a fake boa constrictor wound around his groin. Someone is even wearing their pet rat as a brooch. I'm worried that the dachshund will eat it.

The transvestite is a beautiful pony. He wears a skintight ponyskin bodysuit, and pony head hat, the neck of which is rather like a knight's helmet, through which his beautiful face (painted as a woman's tonight) can peer. A long glossy black tail swishes behind him as he trots superciliously across the dance floor. I am amazed by this outfit. I wonder who made it and what he had to do to get them to make it for him.

The transvestite's boy has dressed as a dalmatian. His outfit is simple – he has bought a skintight white full body leotard and used a permanent marker to ink spots all over it. It is designed to be ridiculous while still showing off his perfect body, the body that is really his life's work. He hasn't bothered to get anything to cover his head. That would get in the way of drinking, and anyhow no-one is going to look at his face.

Next to these splendid creatures, I am under-dressed in my feathers. But I don't care. I don't care about how beautiful or not I am, how wild or not the party is, how magnificent the guests, how the champagne sparkles or the music beats. Everything feels tawdry because my sheets have been ripped by a rotting man, because this time the man who stands to one side at this party, watching me with a nervous but propriatorial smile, is not someone whose admiration I want. I see now that he is a fool, a weakling, a project gone wrong. Gone wrong because, now the sheets have torn, I realize that he is not going to get stronger with me, that he will only continue to dissolve into phlegm and breathlessness until he runs into a stain on my mattress. The sort of stain that won't be scrubbed out.

I move around the party digesting this new vision.

I am not really here. Neither, I think, are the boys. But unlike me they are trying. The transvestite continues to shake his mane to the beat while the boy staggers around beautifully, telling foolish jokes and drinking from two of the rental champagne flutes at once. But they are lacklustre despite their sharp beauty. I stand at the edge of the room, as far away from the grey man as possible, and watch my boys, my beautiful boys, who seem to have had the life drained from them. I think that they, like me, are suffocated by the grey man, by the miasma that he seems to drag behind him, that has seeped out of my bedroom and into the flat, somehow blighting their lives too.

Even the guests are affected. They seem sluggish, bored, almost somnambulant, despite the fact that I have seen a steady train of them shuffle across the bridge into my bedroom, where I know that the grey man is racking out line after

line of cocaine and the guests are bending over my
gold mirror to hoover it up. Perhaps they are
hoovering up desperation and dissolution with it, I
think. Mould and phlegm and crumbling plaster.
Perhaps that is what he is giving them, the
mouldering room and his mouldering life ground
up and laid out for them as if it were something
beautiful, precious, that could make their hearts
dance.

I go in to see what is happening, and find him
sitting on the bed with another man, one of my
guests, someone I know vaguely. The other man is
dressed as a fox, though his costume is askew and
unconvincing. The grey man has taken his
squirrel's ears off but his tail is still attached and
springs up absurdly behind his head. My lovely
gold mirror sits between them, smeared with
white powder.

The music from the party is loud enough to
make even this distant room throb, but there is
sudden pause while one boy or the other decides
what to play next.

Both men look at me in the silence. Their eyes
are equally empty, although somewhere in the
grey man's emptiness, I glimpse fear. As if he

knows how vulnerable he is to me.

The music starts to thud again and I leave them to it.

I try to dance but his presence gnaws at me, makes me miss the beat. No one is dancing well – whatever he is giving the other guests is not having the usual effect on their dancing feet. No one tries to be spectacular, no one writhes or stomps or winds. Couples do not meet for the first time in joyous explosion on this dance floor; old friends do not explore the eroticism of their familiarity, their bone old ties; enemies do not surprise themselves with their shared ecstasy. Instead we all shuffle like the undead, our gazes lowered and our fists clenched, wondering whether it would be impolite to go home, go to bed, give up. It is insufferable.

I manage to drag my eyes from the floor long enough to catch the eyes with the transvestite. He raises his eyebrows at me from deep within the horse's neck. He is challenging me. I know what he means.

The grey man must be erased from our lives.

I go back to the bedroom.

"Darling," he says, hopefully.

"You must leave now," I say. "We don't want you here any more. We can't bear it."

He starts to cry and I think that he may never stop. So in order to help him stop, I tell him that I have never properly loved him, that I have let him stay because I wanted to help him, wanted to make him strong but I cannot bear his weakness and disease any longer. Cannot bear to have him rotting away in my room, staining and tearing my life, the life of my boys, my world.

This works and he stops crying and starts shouting. I don't care because I am so relieved to have said it, to have the power to make him go. I lie back against the pillows on the gold bed and let his outrage wash over me.

Eventually even this runs out and he sits in silence, slumped on the edge of the bed.

"Please leave," I say quietly. And he does, taking almost nothing with him. I feel sorry at the thought of him walking out through the party into the night, walking to nowhere, into the four winds. But his nothing is no longer my business, and after he walks out of the room I think of nothing, but just lie in the gold bed and feel all my muscles unclench.

I stroke the fine worn patch of sheet around the tear and the party music thuds on funereally as I slip into sleep.

The End

I meet Tall Paul at a party. I am taken to the party by Billy, an eccentric man who owns a huge wolfhound bitch. Billy says he likes me because I am old. He says that all his girlfriends are incredibly young, and he complains that they are boring and foolish. He runs nightclubs and I suppose that nightclubs are all full of young women, so it is not surprising that this is what he ends up with. He says that they fling themselves at him and he is apparently unable to resist them. He is more than a little mad, so I am not sure whether anyone who was not crazed by youth could put up with him.

Billy lives in the East of the city in an area full of bars and clubs and restaurants. When he walks around his bitch follows him carefully. She never wears a lead. If he goes somewhere that doesn't allow dogs she simply sits outside and waits until he emerges. She seems quite safe. Probably no one would dare try and kidnap such a vast animal.

I think that the bitch is so obedient because he is such a distracted man. He pays her very little attention, which is the perfect way to subordinate a dog. I suppose that he has the same effect on the young women.

Billy and I kiss a few times but although I admire his eccentricity, his dog and his very sweet nature (he perpetually seems bewildered by life and craves affection). I find his vagueness off-putting. It is as if a part of him is missing. I think perhaps he did a few too many drugs in his youth. But still he is a faithful friend.

The party is in a warehouse at the edge of a five-lane concrete highway to the east of the city. Billy drives me there in an ancient 1930s maroon truck that he bought on eBay. It seems quite a fragile vehicle and I wonder if it will get us there. We get lost on the way, have to wind our way through depressing residential streets which are too dirty and of the city to be suburban, even though they are miles away from the centre of town. Eventually we find our way onto the highway, and then get lost again, as we cannot find an exit, although our map tells us that there should be one near the warehouse. Billy gets a little plaintive but I don't mind the getting lost. I am wearing a pretty dress and my lips are painted red and in my head I am already at the party being admired.

We get there an hour later than we planned. The party is being thrown by an artist, one famous enough that I recognize his name, though I have no idea what his work is like. The warehouse is full of random things – props and old furniture and old lamps. No art.

It is also full of people that I have never met who all seem to know one another. They are happy and relaxed and look interesting but I am struck by shyness. I shadow Billy around as he twirls his moustache and laughs his fruity laugh. He is consummately at ease at a party, a club, any night-time activity. I resign myself to a night attached to his coattails and start to drink the bottle of champagne that we have bought with us. I want some Dutch courage.

Eventually I am drunk enough to dance by myself. A Mexican band is playing and I twirl and flounce around the dance-floor. The other dancers are friendly, join in with my dance so I feel better, less lonely, inspired to dance more extravagantly. I do not need to hang on to Billy's coat tails. I can dance. I swing my hips and angle my shoulders and imagine that I am being watched and admired by everyone else in the warehouse, though when I look around I see that they are almost all lost in their own conversations and dances. I shake myself and pay more attention to the dance itself, the pleasure of moving my body to the music rather than the pleasure of display.

Then I get tired and feel myself starting to sober up, so I make my way to a large table covered in bottles and hunt down something that I can drink. A tall skinny man with dark hair joins me at the table, also hunting for unemptied bottles. He is wearing black clothes, elegant and simple. I immediately like him. I am bold after my dance so talking is easy. He seems sweet, gentle, a little naughty. He tells me that he and his friends have been taking cocaine then giggles. We find the remains of a bottle of vodka and share it. After a few swigs we start flirting and I find that he is very funny.

An hour later, the party is flagging so he takes me home in a taxi to his flat. His name is Paul.

Before we leave, I kiss Billy goodbye. He looks a little disappointed.

I wake up in the early morning, before dawn. I have a headache and feel battered by alcohol and sex and exhaustion. I am in Paul's flat which is a large concrete box with small windows set high in the walls, everything in one room, including the desk where he works which has an enormous white computer monitor on it, and his kitchen which is a mess of half-drunk bottles.

Most of these were already here when I arrived a few hours ago, drunk and excited at the thought of another adventure. His record collection stretches across the room in specially made plywood shelving. The collection is all vinyl.

The naked concrete walls are lit by street-lamps that shine through the high windows. I wander around in this cold half light, not enjoying the feeling of rough sisal carpet under my bare feet. I am hunting for a clean glass, for painkillers. I find neither in the kitchen area. I find the bathroom which is also concrete and sparse, but there is a ledge covered with fancy lotions and creams and

cleansers so I wash my face, wash off the dark
stains of kohl and mascara and hope that I will
still look beautiful without them when the sun
comes up. There is also a small set of wire drawers
full of razors and cotton wool and at the bottom of
this I find paracetamol which is my painkiller of
choice, so I am happy.

I climb back into bed and Paul wraps his long
arms around me. His arms and torso are so long
that I feel completely enfolded by them. It is a
pleasant feeling but I cannot sleep. The aches keep
me awake, and also a feeling of disquiet. The way
he has wrapped himself around me, though
sensual, feels impersonal, an almost robotic
response to my body, to any woman's body. I no
longer think this man is as sweet and gentle. He
did not fuck like a sweet man. It was a hard
impersonal fuck, intense and almost frenzied.
Nothing to do with me or sweetness. I did not
enjoy it though I was impressed by the size of his
cock.

After such a fuck, I do not feel safe and I would
like to leave. But somehow creeping off in the dark
seems too harsh. So I stay, awake, staring at the
light cast on the concrete walls.

Many hours later, Paul wakes up. He smiles briefly at me, pulls on his jeans and goes to the bathroom. I sit huddled in his bedcovers, using them as protection.

I am surprised when he casually slides back into bed and slips an arm around me. He seems relaxed, but still distant considering that just hours ago we were fucking.

I suddenly understand that all his gestures are automatic – the fucking, the holding, the arm around my shoulder. An automatic response to a female body.

I wriggle out of his casually slung arm and ask him how many women he has fucked in the last week.

"You know, I'm not sure. I think probably about nine."

I laugh.

We start to talk and he shows me some astonishing Japanese cartoon porn on his huge computer screen.

It turns out that he is fucking all of these women because his heart has been completely broken by one. She was a model, so he hunts for model types. I am flattered when I realise this, though I think there were slim pickings at the party and I must have just been preferable to an empty bed. He needed a torso to penetrate and hold onto. The model had a tiny daughter, not his, but he helped bring her up. He seems to think that this was the most important thing that he has ever done. As we talk, I come to see that losing the little girl is what is really messing him up. Not so easy to replace as a woman's body in your bed.

His voice is soft, almost effeminate, and he has the long curling eyelashes of a cow. His eyes are rich nut brown. Exactly the same colour as mine.

We talk about stories. The first conversation about stories that I have had in a long time. He is a designer but he prefers words and is brimming with stories that he wants to tell and he wants to hear mine too. This feels good.

After a few hours of talk Paul walks me to the underground station. It is a glaringly sunny city day and the traffic and crowds on the streets make my headache more intense. I tell him that I'm not interested in being lovers and he doesn't seem to care. But as we say goodbye he says with great seriousness that he wants us to be friends. So I give him my phone number and make my way through the subway system back to the peace of the white flat. As I am swept down into the station by the escalators I am already dreaming of a day spent buried in the huge sheepskin rug.

I do not think that I will hear from Paul again. He is too bound up in seducing and fucking reams of women. I don't mind as I think I understand. But I think about him. His mind and his ebullient enthusiasm and his interest in stories. In talking about making new things, new stories. Our meeting has made me want to write, made me want to finally write my own stories down, stories that I have been planning to write for years.

I feel stories start to bubble up in me. I start to see how many stories I have lived, to think how these could be shaped into patterns that make sense of things. Sense of the years that I have abandoned, allowing them to be taken over by other people, people to whom I have subjugated myself. Patterns that are woven into me but now I find I can also float above, mapping and twisting as I please. I feel that stories might transform me into something new. I sit in my damp white basement feeling full of light as patterns form in my mind. I catch them and write them down in a large, black hard-bound notebook.

I stop hunting men.

While I am catching stories, I see a Venetian masquerade in a film on the TV. It excites me and I convince the boys that we should throw our own masked party. We become very excited about this – even more excited than we usually are about parties. It seems that we all want to be something new. Something other.

I send Paul an invitation by text message. His phone number is the only way I have of contacting him. I cannot remember where he lives.

I don't hear back from him.

For some reason I prepare myself for the party with more care and attention to detail than usual, even though I have no desire to seduce. I scrub and shave my body until it is white marble, have my hairdresser put up my hair in an elaborate chignon laced about with little plaits, cover every inch of my face with careful painting although much of it will be hidden by the mask. I have chosen a black half mask with a fringe of long black feathers winging out from its sides. Below it my lips are a carefully drawn blood-red bow. My dress is voluminous, many layers of black silk chiffon with more feathers at the wrists and hems. The dress entirely hides my body except for my shoulders and throat which are white and uncovered. I am pleased with the final effect. My disguise is disguise. I am hidden.

The transvestite has made his own mask. It has two halves. The right side of its face is brutish and masculine and has a dark curling moustache (made of real hair glued on curl by curl – I do not want to think about where he got it from). The left side of the mask is lascivious and female, with lips even redder than mine, a beauty spot, lined eyes and feathery false lashes. He has also made a wig to go with the mask – has sewn together half a wig of short curling black hair for his masculine side, and a half of tumbling red curls for the feminine. Seen from the either side, he is a convincing lothario or temptress. From the front he is terrifying.

The Boy is less interested in the masking. He wears a full-faced cheap plastic Joker mask, which

I know will spend most of the evening perched on top of his head so that he can drink his fill.

So here we are. A shadow, an ambivalent and a joke. We laugh delightedly.

The guests start to arrive and, since I am shadow, I hide in the dark corners of our small outdoor space and watch as masks walk down the dark steps to our basement and reveal themselves in the light. An ice queen and two square-headed silver robots arrive first. They look a little dazed but the Joker Boy whisks them inside and presses champagne into their silvery gloves.

A dog comes next, with a fake fur face and whiskers that quiver in the night wind. He trots happily into the light as the transvestite starts up the music. A pierrot looms into view in the darkness, his or her white face glowing, waiting for something or someone. A fat Buddha joins the pierrot and they lock arms and dance down the steps. Later, I see them kissing passionately on the dance floor. The moon arrives next, accompanied by a tiny person wearing a vast sun mask, its rays almost reaching the floor in one direction, doubling his height in the other.

On and on they come, more guests than we

have ever entertained here in the basement. I
think I recognize one or two, but we have warned
them all in their invitation that to take off their
mask is against the rules, that they will be sent
home if they do, so I am not sure if I know anyone
here. I keep watching.

Once the flat is full of people, I feel it is safe to
emerge from the shadows because now I can slip
between the other masks unnoticed. I feel
wonderfully free. The champagne starts to bubble
in my veins. As it does I become bolder and seek
out the masks that I think are the most beautiful –
a unicorn with a sad princess, a cubist *femme
fatale* – and whisper my admiration to them. But I
avoid conversation. I do not need to be hostess.
The boy miraculously keeps everyone's glasses full
and the transvestite keeps the music going,
playing weird and exciting songs that I have not
heard before. And the masks are doing their job,
giving their wearers courage and something to talk
about, even to total strangers who they cannot see.

There are stories everywhere here tonight. The
Buddha talks to a demon with three faces. The dog
asks the sad princess to dance. The transvestite
makes the moon kiss his temptress face while the

sun reaches up and fondles his half moustache. The unicorn leans drunkenly against a tree glowering jealously at the princess. A demon is bent over the rabbit cage, clucking affectionately.

The rabbits seem in their element. They are both lying stretched long on their hay, noses trembling, their ears following the noises of the party like radars. They glow in the half light, and look for all the world as if they know that their costumes are the best, that (unlike the poor humans) they are always dressed as magnificent wild things.

We have put the parrots to bed by covering their cage with a dark cloth but they are being kept awake by the music and are frustrated. They make insistent low whistles, and when these are ignored they start to shriek. But they are hardly heard over the music and hubbub so eventually they climb down the inside of their cage to where the cloth does not quite cover the bottom of the cage and peer out at us.

The boy sees them there and takes pity on them and pulls off the cloth. They climb rapidly up the cage again, the parrot claw-and-beak climb, and sit mesmerised on their perches. They are silent and enthralled for the rest of the night.

Two men arrive in simple cardboard masks. One is a Red Indian Chief, the other Nelson or Napoleon – I can't tell which. The masks completely cover their faces except for their eyes which shine blackly through the eye-holes. Other than the masks the men are in modern, ordinary clothes, quite elegant. One man is broad and muscled, like a public school rugby player. The other is tall, rangy, long-boned.

I watch them from behind the group of masks that are gathered by the oak table, which is still loaded with bottles of champagne. They whisper and giggle.

The Cure is playing on the stereo:

And she used to fall down a lot
That girl was always falling
Again and again...

"Hello," says a soft, amused voice behind me. A tall voice from behind a mask of Napoleon or Nelson, I can't tell which. "I know who you are".

"I think I know who you are too."

"That's very satisfactory."

"I'm surprised that you are here."

"I am so sorry that I disappeared. Are you really surprised though?"

"Perhaps not."

We dance together gently, Paul and I, who tonight is Admiral, Emperor or Lord. It is like dancing with a reed in the wind. Then he passes me gently to the Red Indian, who by contrast is solid like a tree.

When I am tired, we drift outside into my garden of shadows, all three of us together, and talk.

The Red Indian is George. He is an artist. "George is very young and has just split up with his first ever girlfriend," says Paul. "They've been together since he was seventeen and now he's feeling lost and frightened. I'm trying to make him feel excited and free."

"Can you imagine being excited to be free?" I ask.

"I am always excited. Frightened too but excited."

"I think you are over-excited. I think you are a little hysterical. Perhaps George is right to be frightened."

"What do you think George? Are you right to be frightened?"

"I am frightened that I will become a hunter like you."

"Why is that frightening?"

"I don't want to start falling into the arms of a string of women."

"Why not?"

"I think they might eat me, or I might eat them."

Paul and I laugh long and hard.

The party is starting to decay. The guests are tired of the masquerade and pull off their masks, revealing sweaty human faces. They still dance but the magic is no longer strong.

My lipstick faded long ago but I keep my mask on. The transvestite still wears his, though the boy's plastic face has been trampled on the dance floor. The boy is very drunk and dancing as if he is on a sinking ship, lurching from one deck to another. The transvestite tries to get him to go to bed, embarrassed by his stumbling. The boy refuses and lurches on. The transvestite watches him, leaning against one of the white concrete walls and I know him so well that I can see what he is thinking even through his double disguise. Which is not really a disguise, but an expression of what lies beneath his pretty blonde face. The complex creature is revolted by his lover's simple happy drunkenness. The maskless boy is not exquisite or strange enough for him.

The boy notices it too. Through his alcohol fog he senses that he is being scorned. And the next time the transvestite drags him off the dance floor, the boy snarls something vicious up at him. The tall transvestite pauses for a minute, holding his shorter, broader lover at one long arm's length, looking down at him through his male and female eyes. Then his other arm makes a fist and flies at the boy's jaw, and the boy falls. Moments later, blood from his mouth is pooling on the floor.

I wait for a moment to see what the transvestite will do next. He does nothing.

The boy pushes himself up and totters into their bedroom, which is adjacent to the dance floor. I follow him and watch him throw himself onto the bed. I check him over and see that he is not really hurt – only his lip is split.

He does not seem to notice the blood.

I mop it up.

This is not the end of the party. The party doesn't seem to want to end. The music keeps playing and keeps calling us onto the dance floor.

Eventually, only Paul, George, the transvestite and I are left dancing in the white flat. I feel full of love for them all, even the strangely violent transvestite. Our feet hurt now so we stop and fall onto the long black sofa. The music stops.

We sit, still and happy, the party still whirling in our heads.

George and Paul decide to spend the night with me. They pull off their trousers and climb into the huge gold bed. I go into my bathroom and strip off my mask, my makeup and my clothes. I put on my favourite nightdress and climb up the bed and lie between them. Paul reaches for my left hand, and George for my right. I feel supremely safe.

Paul turns out the lights.

Paul falls asleep first. His breathing deepens and starts to rasp. As it does, George leans over and kisses me gently.

"You are very wonderful."

"Thank you. This is all very wonderful."

"I don't know what we are doing here. Do you?"

"I think so."

"Tell me."

"In the morning, perhaps."

Soon, his breathing deepens too. I lie awake listening. I feel as though I am wrapped in the heart of a story.

During the night, Paul flings his arm across me and wraps his long torso around me possessively. I know it is not me that he wants to possess.

In the morning, we wake up laughing.

We feel free like children.

Paul says: "This is the last chapter of your book."

I say: "It is."

Postscript

The problem with writing is that it makes you face things even as you are turning them into other things.

As I finish writing this, my death fear comes back. It comes back late at night when I am alone in my bed. I suddenly remember that death is a terrifying precipice that I will stumble over one day and never return. I am deeply disturbed by this thought. It is a truth more terrifying than any ghost story. I do not sleep well for days.

You may read this when I am dead. Though I doubt that this is a story that will last that long. But, just in case, please know that I once really was alive and now I am dead.

And my words are like the clone of myself that I imagined breeding to fight off death. They are not really me. They cannot do it. They cannot keep me alive beyond my death. But I love them anyway.

And I loved the men.

229

Also from The Real Press:

THE PIPER
David Boyle

It is the summer of 1990. The first Gulf War
looms, the satanic abuse panic rages, and one
strange market town, unchanged for decades,
suddenly and disastrously runs out of money. The
crisis brings together the mayor and the man he
wronged four decades before. This is a haunting
tale of passing time, and a Pied Piper story for our
own era, of the Blitz, the explosion of money, of
clone towns, the Wright Brothers and growing up
– and local currencies. And above it all, stands the
ancient landscape of Dragon Hill.

www.therealpress.co.uk

Printed in Great Britain
by Amazon